Long John Cardinal
and other
Watering Trough Stories

Dalton Roberts

Long John Cardinal
and other
Watering Hole Stories

Dalton Roberts

Chattanooga
Bookmakers

Table of Contacts

Introduction

Anyone who lives long enough will meet a lot of people. If you happened to have started in the newspaper business when you were 17 years old in 1950, you would have met a lot of very interesting people. There was Harry Moore (who claimed he broke the Wright Brothers flight story) and Tem Wicker. Richard Nixon and Sam Ervin. Jersey Joe Walcott and Yogi Berra. John Bubbles and Robert deNiro. Ray Price arid Cristy Lane. And a lot of other folks. After a while you aren't easily impressed.

Dalton Roberts would impress anyone. He was Hamilton County Executive when I came to Chattanooga 20 years ago. He was so forceful and plainspoken I couldn't understand how he not only remained in office, but was as popular as he was. It was because of that bluntness, that dedication to honesty that made him say what the thought and do what he believed right. That's why he was loved or hated. But even when he was hated, it was with respect.

It would seem strange for anyone else to be son of a minister, earning money beginning at the age of 16 picking a guitar and singing in nightclubs. He scrubbed floors to work his way through college and on graduation took a job teaching children with disabilities.

When he ran for office as the first Hamilton County Executive in the newly created office, political advisers told him to stay away from his nightclub friends. He said if he had to turn his back on friends he had rather not be in politics. Those friends helped put him in office. His ability and actions earned him the right to stay there as long as he wanted.

He is the most multi-talented person you will ever meet. A politician and public servant. A stand up entertainer with music and commentary in the manner of a Mark Twain or Lewis Grizzard. He can preach a sermon in a church or let his hair down and party with the good ole boys. Whatever he does, he does well.

Last but certainly not least is his talent as a writer. He has the ability to fashion words together to capture the imagination and heart of the reader. Sometimes he serves a view universally familiar in a new light. Sometimes he takes the mind down a new path.

In another time and place, he might have been defending Galileo's right to study the stars. He might have served as a general fighting Napoleon at Waterloo. In Bloody Kansas before the Civil War, he could have been preaching against the evils of slavery.

He would always have been there against hypocrisy, corruption and anyone or anything seeking to enslave the freedom of the mind.

His quest for truth and bringing that light into dark corners comes through in his writing. Each piece delivers a tantalizingly different thought. Most difficult part of putting this collection together was taking detours to read or reread a column.

Pete Chaney
Chattanooga, TN
January 2006

Preface

The most common request when I entertain community groups is for a book of my best columns. The one column they mention most frequently is the one about my one-legged redbird friend, Long John Cardinal.

I have bonded with a couple of dogs I have owned and one cat. I even bonded with a hog snake that came daily to eat aphids in my garden. But Long John is my favorite animal pal of all.

I sought the opinion of my readers about the columns to feature in this collection and included as many of those favorites as space allowed. In fact, I've got enough favorites to do a couple more bookazines! Hopefully, we will be able to do that in time.

When Ron Smith and Paul Neely asked me in 1994 to write a column for the Chattanooga Times, I had no good idea of how I would like doing it. I had always loved writing songs but had not done any column writing. I was leaving a full-time job and did not want to immediately tie myself down with new responsibilities.

However, I agreed to do it and I am glad I did.

Why? One of the big reasons is that it keeps me in touch with the people. I missed that daily feedback from the people when I left politics. It helped me to steer the county in a good direction. To my pleasure I have discovered that a column brings the same kind of feedback.

Another reason is that writing is an unending

challenge. I have always needed a job that kept me on tiptoes.

Like teaching children with learning disorders or running a county government. I have found that writing is as much of a challenge as anything I have done.

Like most writers, I have had a lifetime love affair with words. Decades before I wrote that first column I had bought all kinds of books on word origins, word usage, word collections and a long row of quotation books. Any songwriter is a word nut and I have written songs most of my life.

Without Tom Griscom this collection might not have ever been put together. When he came home to manage the Times Free Press he asked me to come off the editorial page and do my thing in the Life section of the paper.

I do not have a deep enough interest in politics to print a book of my political columns but appearing in the Life section gave me the philosophical elbow room I needed to soar off into any subject that fascinated me. I am grateful to Tom for seeing that I had more to offer than political commentary.

Most of the columns in this collection came from the Chattanooga Times and the Chattanooga Times Free Press and the rest of them came from My Sunday Journal, a Sunday inspirational column I have written for International Press Service Features the past few years. My friend, Pete Chaney, developed IPS several decades ago but we added the IPS Features to make some good writers available to newspapers all over the world.

My precious mother, Nora Woodall Roberts, graced my life for 56 years with her wit, spirituality, keen intellect and insatiable appetite for words. She was an excellent poet and novelist and no matter where my travels took me, her long, sparkling letters brightened my days. I remember the look of ecstasy that came across her face when she was writing. Sometimes I feel that she is still writing through me. I miss her but I am fortunate to have hundreds of her letters and poems in the pages of my personal journal. Through those words, she continues to watch over my soul like she did when she made the Spirit of God real to me when I was a small boy.

I offer these words in the hope that they will inspire, challenge and entertain my readers half as much as my mothers words and the words of so many great writers have inspired, challenged and entertained me. If anything is better for the mind and soul than reading, I have not yet discovered it.

Dalton Roberts
Downtown Watering Trough
January 2006

Swap Rubber Stamps for Eagle Wings

Now and then I set aside a day to get rid of my rubber stamp. Not the rubber stamp I have found to be useful in handling my mail but the one I use to stamp my days. I wrote about it in a poem:

> *Days can become rubber stamps*
> *relentlessly pounding out*
> *the same impressions*
> *on our lives.*
> *The same alarm clock*
> *jarring us*
> *to the same outlook*
> *on the same things.*
> *The same bar of soap*
> *shampoo*
> *socks*
> *and suit of clothes.*
> *The same car*
> *on the lockstep route*
> *to the cluttered office*
> *and the same unsolved problems.*
> *The same people*
> *chewing up minds*
> *and time*

with the same things.
The same route home
among squirming cars
teeth clenched
radios jangling.
The same unhappy
happy hours
chatter mounting
as loneliness drinks

Get the idea? We can allow our lives to become monotonous litanies, boring folderol, rigor mortis rituals, each new day a rubber-stamp of the day before.

When I was a teenager, I saved my money and bought an A-Model Ford. Dad put hydraulic brakes on it rather than the mechanical brakes that took a football field to come to a stop. My cousin and I painted it. It was mighty good at attracting female companions but what I loved most about it was I could keep it going with a screwdriver.

There wasn't much to go wrong on an A-Model except the timing and I could pop off one little cap and take my screwdriver with the motor idling and tune that sucker until it purred like a fresh-fed kitten.

That's all I am suggesting we do with the days of our life. Just tune them up a little more to our highest values. See if there are some people we've outgrown and need to tune out. See if there are some exciting new acquaintances we need to tune in and really get to know.

One-third of our life is spent on a job so see if you need to tune up your present job or tune it out. One-third is spent in activities of our choice and we may want to spend less time building a beer belly in a recliner and a little more mowing the grass at our church or for some widow down the street struggling to make ends meet on a small Social Security check.

The remaining one-third of our time is spent sleeping and I can tell you from recent experience how important that third can be and how easy it might be to tune it up. Since a whiplash in 1977, I have spent a small fortune on chiropractors. As a large gamble, I paid $100 for a Tempurpedic pillow. I was not optimistic because I have tried at least a dozen pillows in recent years but this was a bingo! It has reduced my chiropractic visits and made sleeping as pleasurable as when I was a kid. Yes, I know that is a lot to spend on a pillow but I am talking about the quality of one-third of my life.

The goal is not to sell Tempurpedic pillows but to attune your mind to the immense difference one small change can make in your life this year.

I started this column with my poem initially titled "Rubberstamp Days" but later changed to "Eagle Wing Days," Let me give you the rest of that poem because it tells about taking the screwdriver of attitude to the A-Model of your life and converting it from a rubber stamp into eagle wings:

But I have known
memorable days
on eagle wings -
riding magical moments.
I ran
and caught the wind
in the sails
of my soul
Somewhere high
in the bluest part of the sky
I dropped my rubberstamp
and flew away.

I wish eagle-wing days for you. So keep that screwdriver handy all the time.

The Pleasure of Prayer Walk

Would you like an activity that can connect your mind and heart to your two good legs - something that will help you get away from it all so you can find it all? Something that will help you grow physically as well as spiritually? Units Mundy says prayer-walking can do all this for you.

You may remember that I wrote a recent column on walking in the rain. Anything that makes me enjoy walking more, I am ready for. And I've never spent five bucks more wisely than buying Mundy's little Abbey Press book titled *Prayer-Walking, A Simple Path to Body and Mind Fitness*. I read it in an hour and it's a ton of fun to try out his ideas.

My first experience of it created a flashback to my high school days when I played hooky one day and walked the area where two large branches feed into South Chickamauga Creek and make a "Y." In fact, everyone in King's Point called it "the Y." I don't recommend that anyone play hooky to take an all-day walk but I will say it was my most creative day of playing hooky. In fact, it was a spiritual feast.

Toward the end of that day I made a bed on pine needles and lay quietly for hours, listening to the wind in the trees. When I read this statement from Catholic mystic Thomas Merton in Mundy's little book, it brought back the smell of the pines and the sound of the wind in the trees: "No writing on the solitary, meditative dimension of life can say anything that has not always been said better by the wind in the pine trees."

Talking about his early prayer-walking, Mundy says "My culture made me do it...we have jammed busy-busy doings into all the nooks and crannies of life...if we can do two things at once, we do." And this gave him a chance to exercise and pray at the same time.

Beware lest this thought makes you think you can prayer-walk like fighting fire, Such an approach kills the spiritual benefits. He quotes Thoreau, "I have met one or two Persons in the course of my life who understood the art of walking...who had the genius for sauntering."

Sauntering. That's it. The day I played hooky was an all-day saunter.

At the same time I was reading Mundy's little jewel, I was also reading *A Poetry Handbook* by the wonderfully gifted poet, Mary Oliver. What she said about taking long saunters when writing a poem fits right in: "Poems can connect the conscious mind and the heart." That's why they contain so much spiritual power. She adds, "Poems are fire for the cold, ropes let down to the lost, and bread in the pockets of the hungry."

Naman Crowe sent me scouring for my poetry books a few years ago talking about the same thing. The more I thought about his words, the more I realized how certain poems had been like Velcro in my mind all the way back to childhood. My mother had a little plastic wall hanging with a poem by Elizabeth Cheney: "Said the Robin to the Sparrow, I should really like to know, why these anxious human being rush about and worry so. Said the Sparrow to the Robin, friend I think that it must be, that they have no heavenly Father, such as cares for you and me."

So if you do some prayer-walking, take along a poem you like and memorize it. Or write one.

Mundy recommends taking a walking stick, a note-book, some spiritual writing for a reading stop under a big tree, some music or "most often, nothing at all."

The main thing, according to Oliver, is to take a walk but don't go anywhere.

Mundy says "something becomes a habit when you do it three times. Maybe just one time if it was fun." One time and I was hooked.

We Need Somebody with Skin

If I had one wish for humanity it would not be for something flashy and spectacular It would be a simple wish that every man, woman and child would realize the value of just being a kind human being.

My Indiana Quaker friend Mariellen Gilpin tells a beautiful story about a little girl being tucked into bed by her father_ When he turned out the lights to leave the room, the child felt a little insecure and called to her father to come back. He assured her, "Go to sleep. God is with you."

In a short while she called for her father again and once again he told her to go to sleep, assuring her God was with her. She said, "Daddy, I know God is with me but right now I want somebody with skin."

Beginning in infancy we develop a skin hunger for the human touch. Studies have shown that babies who are touched and hugged develop psychomotor skills quicker than those who are merely fed. They also develop higher intelligence. In graduate school I recall reading a startling study saying the same thing is true of monkeys. Those who were nursed by their mothers and touched a lot grew up to be less aggressive and violent.

If this early need for gentle human touching has such momentous consequences in later life, isn't it logical to believe it is just as important to us at all other stages of life?

Lewis Grizzard was basically a humorist but once when his mother was very ill he wrote a column that profoundly touched me. He'd been watching some televangelist's healing service and felt there was a lot of insincerity and oven phoniness in it. Then he went to the hospital to see his mother and her Methodist pastor came in. He held and patted her hand, talked quietly with her, then prayed a simple loving prayer. It did for her what the pain pills couldn't do. It eased her peacefully into sleep.

Isn't that something we can all do for one another? Even if you are self-conscious about praying aloud, you can hold someone's hand and tell him or her you care. How many times has "I love you" kept you going when you were sitting on your axle?

We sit around waiting for some bright light to shine down on us and knock us off our old camel. We listen for a mighty rushing wind. We wait for a pillar of fire to go before us. But the power has always been in the still, small voice. No one has yet improved on the kind touch of a human hand.

In his 100th year of life Scott Nearing summarized what he thought was important in this life: "Do the thing you believe in. Do the best you can in the place where you are and be kind."

In today's atmosphere of continuous expectation and fear of terrorist acts, we will have a tendency to become vindictive and uncaring. We must remember that we are all we've got Alice Walker writes in Anything We Love Can Be Saved, "Our last five minutes on earth are running out. We can spend those minutes in meanness, exclusivity and self-righteous disparagement of those who are different from us, or we can spend them consciously embracing every glowing soul who wanders within our reach." I am not certain we are in our last five minutes on earth but I am confident her advice will work to everyone's benefit.

We do not realize the power we possess - the simple supremacy of our kindness. George Herron reminds us: "If the instinctual and repressed kindness of mankind were suddenly let loose upon the earth sooner than we think would we be...singing the song of a new humanity."

We are not helpless. We have kindness. We are not alone. We have each other. Like the little girl told her father we need somebody with human skin.

Don't Mail Rocks and Sticks

In these days of regular orange terror alerts, I would not recommend that you try to mail rocks or sticks. It almost got me hauled off to Gauntanamo Bay.

My sister had the flu and asked me to mail a rock to her friend in Suches, Georgia. Not thinking of how I was dressed (toboggan and combat coat), I dutifully toted it up to the counter at the main post office. The girl asked, "Does this contain anything flammable, fragile, " etc. I cannot remember the long line of adjectives she laid on me but I just said, "No, it's a rock."

My sister paints beautiful scenes on flat rocks and gives them to friends as gifts. It is a great little handicraft idea but not ideally suited for mailing.

The girl at the counter said, "I beg your pardon, sir?"

"A rock," I repeated, getting the same quizzical look from her.

Seeing the fear in her eyes, I quickly realized I had better explain: "A painted rock," I assured her, as if this would resolve her concerns.

I saw her look around like she was scanning the area for a security guard or her supervisor so I added, "A decorated rock."

She walked back behind the barrier separating the mail operations from customers and in a few moments I noticed a man peeking around like a rabbit in a hole. However, she returned to the cubicle and told me I owed her $5.30.

As if she hadn't gotten me in enough trouble with the rock caper, Sis asked me in a few days to mail a box of sticks to another friend. These were not ordinary sticks, mind you. She explained they were for boring holes to hold candles. Why this friend couldn't go out and find her own sticks is a matter I must wonder about but my sister is a little older than I and before I was old enough to go to school she had taught me not to question her about anything. How many times would you have to get your jaws smacked to stop asking questions?

Obediently I took the box of sticks back to the post office. Fate has never been a real close friend of mine so fate saw to it that I got the same counter girl for the sticks I had gotten for the rock. She went through the spiel asking if it contained anything flammable, fragile and I believe'this time she added "explodable." I answered, "No it's just sticks."

A look of terror crossed her face. "Sticks of what?" she asked_ I said, "Just plain old sticks" and suddenly the depths of my dumbness were caressed by the situation. Here I was in that same old combat jacket and had just seen on television an hour earlier that the boys in Homeland Insecurity had taken people from jerking to quivering with a fresh new orange alert. So I immediately said, "Oh, not dynamite in case that's what you were thinking. Just plain sticks to be bored with holes."

"Holes for what? she asked, stepping back from the package as if it might explode in her face at any moment. I said, "Candles! Just plain, simple candles. It's a handcraft thing my sister and her friends have going. And I know they are doing it across state lines so maybe we should call in the FBI."

I started to tell her my sister had the flu and she might ought to check it for viruses and germs but people in the long Christmas line were getting restless. I decided to be a real sweet guy. I became appropriately humble and cooperative.

My unabashed honesty and sweet little innocent face finally got through to her and saved the day.

I know my sister could go back to smacking my jaws at any time but if she ever needs any more rocks or sticks mailed, she will do it herself.

Some Interesting Preachers I've Known

You May not believe my stories about preachers I have known but they are all true. Some of them are so wild you are bound to know I could not have made them up.

I wrote about a preacher named Jewett in my first book. He was a former moonshine runner in Kentucky. One night he lost control of his car. It turned over on him as the load of moonshine went into flames He lost an arm and a leg. He figured this was God's way of calling him to preach.

He would walk all over the church when he preached, flailing the air with his one good arm, his artificial leg making creaking sounds as he walked and yelled.

One night a woman in a pew had one of those old-time hearing aids with a volume control on it. Jewett noticed that she would turn the volume off when he touched on her favorite sins. He creaked his way over to her and stood right in front of her moving his lips but saying nothing. She thought her hearing aid had died and tapped it a couple of times, then turned the volume up full blast. Jewett screamed at her, "Don't you ever turn me off when I am preaching the truth, sister!" She came a foot off the pew and probably lost the rest of her hearing.

Then there was a preacher I will just call "Pew

Walker" because he loved to walk the backs of pews. He was skinny and wore suspenders attached to britches at least two inches larger than his waist. He would stick his thumbs down in his britches and pull them down several inches as he preached and when he released his thumbs his pants would jiggle up and down.

One Sunday morning in a revival he ran and started walking the pews, working his way through a half dozen when he noticed a huge chandelier hanging slightly beyond the altar. It was more than he could stand. He took a running shot from the platform to the altar, ricocheting upward, grabbing the chandelier and swinging out over the congregation. It, would have been some feat had the chandelier not come loose and crashed down in the center aisle of the church, sending glass flying in every direction. Once again someone rushed up and asked, "Are you alright?" and once again he yelled, "Stand back! If I hadn't been out of the will of God, I would not have fallen!"

The wildest one of all had the nickname of "Hawk" due to his large eyeballs and penetrating stare. On one occasion he actually hid some chains near the main light switch of a church. He preached his way back to the light switch, turned off the lights, and went down the aisles telling how the devil would chain all the unsaved in the bottomless pits of hell. When the lights came back on, half the congregation was at the altar.

One Sunday morning I heard him preach on "What-soever you do, do all to the glory of God." He said, "Even if you tiptoe, do it for Jesus." He quietly tiptoed all the way across the front of the church. Then he said, "I want someone to volunteer to join me and tiptoe for Jesus." No one did so he grabbed a little mousy-looking man and dragged him out of a pew while the little man screamed,

"Oh no! Please!" Together they silently tiptoed around the front of the church.

I loved them all. Their antics kept this preacher's kid from the jaws of boredom.

Becoming Content is Achievable

It matters not how much you achieve or how much money you make if you don't find contentment. Yet there appears to be a conspiracy against contentment.

Television is constantly goading us to get up and do something to make ourselves look better, cook better, feel better or smell better. Contentment with what we are and how we smell is out of the question.

In one week's mail I have gotten a half dozen powerful urges to attend workshops or to read books that prick and prod one to set higher goals or to focus on saving the world. If you have found contentment get ready to be blitzed by those with a bias against bliss.

There is certainly a time in life for goal setting but there is also a time to set our goals aside. Most of the hours of our days and nights we need to set our minds to the pleasures we are enjoying or the projects on our work tables. To constantly be whipping ourselves like a horse to run faster and faster actually works against doing well on what we are doing. But the larger issue is that it keeps us from squeezing the joy juice out of the orange of today.

Shinzen Young teaches a meditation method he calls "slow movement." It is very simple; just slow down no matter what you are doing. I mean half speed. If you are washing dishes, intentionally go very slow. You will have to keep slowing down because after only seconds of slowing down, you will find yourself speeding up. Stay with it and do it often for it can im-merse you in the moment in a powerful way.

Yes, it is simple but that does not mean it is easy. The one and only difficulty with it is our habitual frenzied pace of living. Experiment with it and you will see. The first time you do it, you will experience a keen awareness of deep relaxation. Despite that reward, you will not find it easier to do the second time. Old habits die slowly and they scream and cuss you a lot while they are croaking.

I think this run run, push push, grab grab, climb climb thing is mainly something we Americans have inflicted upon ourselves. A beautiful Internet story makes this point in telling about an American docking his boat in a Mexican coastal village and complimenting a Mexican fisherman on the quality of his catch. "How long did it take you to catch them?" he asked the Mexican.

"Not very long," the Mexican replied.

"Then why don't you devote more time to it and make more money?" the American wondered.

"Well," the Mexican answered, "I catch enough to provide a good living for my family. I sleep late, play with my children, take a nap with my wife and in the evenings I go into the village to see my friends, have a few drinks, play my guitar and sing a few songs."

The American with his MBA from Harvard offered to help the Mexican, assuring him he could help him build a fleet of trawlers and establish a booming fish business, then sell it all for millions. The Mexican asked, "After that, what?"

The American said, "Oh, it will be wonderful! You will be able to retire when you are an old man. You can sleep late, play with your children, take a nap with your wife, and go into town in the evenings to see your friends, have a few drinks, play your guitar and sing a few songs."

This one made me chuckle but it also made me look at all the great things I am able to enjoy right now and every day of my life - things that bring deep contentment. Getting rich and famous is not a prerequisite for contentment. As Barney Morgan used to say, "My refrigerator will get my milk as cold as any rich man's."

Questions for Times of Change

Five hundred years before Christ, Heraclitus said, "You cannot go into the same river twice." It sounds silly but he is right because he is talking about change and no matter how many times you walk in the river, it is always different.

Every day you walk out your door, the world is different. Every person you saw yesterday will be different today, some sadder and some happier. Some may even be gone. One day I had lunch with a friend and the next day he died.

One day I knew a man who was scraping out a hard living and the next day he had millions. Some spiritual giants have taught that all change is simply a chance at soul practice. It is easier to believe that when things go to suit us.

I am not a spiritual giant. When something painful crashes into my world, I tend to think of it as "bad." I hope you are a more evolved soul but from my observation most people quickly classify unpleasant experiences that way.

My way of trying to gain growth from setbacks is to ask three questions of each experience. The first is more a request than a question. I simply ask the unpleasant experience to not let me repress it. To keep elbowing me until I think. To repress is to regress. That which we don't express tends to crawl off into our inner being and die. Like a big stinking bubble it pops out when we least expect it and bursts in our face.

The second question I ask in a time of change is, "What good has come of the 'bad' experiences of my life?" You know, those things we quickly chalked up as "bad" when they first slugged us in the pit of the stomach.

If you don't keep a journal it is important to write down the answers to that question. St. Paul called it "stirring up the pure mind by way of remembrance." I call it training my eyes to see what they don't want to see and my ears to hear what they don't want to hear. You will find that many of the things you called "bad" led to transformations and more satisfying situations. Maybe you survived the brutality of the one you thought you couldn't live without, learned how to spot a purveyor of poison and then found someone that respected and cared for you.

Sure there is usually a touch of sadness. Anatole France said, "All changes, even the most longed for, have their melancholy, for what we leave behind us is a part of ourselves." If only we could see those pieces of ourselves we invested in old relationships and situations as seeds that will yield good fruit in due season. Some seeds grow self-esteem for us by knowing we did some things right in a bad situation.

Finally, I ask myself, "What bad has come from. situations I once saw as good?" This one is harder be-cause it requires admitting we were wrong in a loving assumption. However, it can ultimately do you, more good than the other two questions by creating the habit of keeping an eye on our glib and shallow assumptions. One such assumption is thinking someone loves you when they repeat it like a brain-damaged parrot. Until someone walks with you through some rain, stands by you through some pain and puts little feet on big pretty words you can only classify them as neutral. They haven't yet done anything substantial for your happiness and welfare. Self-evident facts like this can get lost in the steam of passion and the smoke of pipe dreaming

Washington Irving summed it up: "There is a certain relief in change even though it is from bad to worse. I have found in traveling in a stage coach that it is often a comfort to shift one's position and be bruised in a new place."

Settle for nothing less the next time you step in the river of change.

We Grow Doing Life's Little Things

True success does not come when we reach some pinnacle of acclaim recognized by society. True success is being able to be deeply fulfilled being small and doing small things.

I love reading the lives of the great mystics and saints of the early Catholic Church. In her young years, Therese aspired to be big. She wanted to be a priest, a deacon, and an apostle - even a martyr. Then she said, "I have found my place ... I shall be love." She called this her "little way." Walking this "little way" enriched her spirit so much that she became one of the most radiant and magnetic influences of her day. Why did her contentment with doing little things have such a powerful mellowing power in her inner spirit? Could it be that this process enabled her to rise above that false sense of self-importance we call ego?

There is a healthy aspect of ego. Freud said ego was the inner instrument for making peace between our lower nature (the id) and our higher values (super-ego). In that sense, it is necessary for us o have a healthy ego. It is the other kind of ego (feeling superior) that can make us miserable. That's what Therese had to plow through to become happy and fulfilled by her "little way." When she chose to make love her way, the very act of being to doing in any small way became a big rainbow-colored bubble of bliss bursting in her inner being.

I have been on top in politics, at least on the local level. It was not easy to get there. It took motivation, exposing myself to the possibility of failure, and sixteen-hour days of campaigning for six months. It took the most intense focus I have ever achieved. I am happy to have had that experience but it has been equally fulfilling to me to go to nursing homes with my guitar and enjoy putting smiles on faces in pain.

How do you compare two experiences so seemingly dissimilar?

The simple truth is that they are not dissimilar at all. Someone has merely convinced us that one is "big" and one is "small." Isn't the higher path to just do what you do as well as you can do it no matter how big or small it may appear to others? When both activities become the same thing to us, we have found a key to happiness.

Why do we classify some things as "small" and speak of them as if they are unimportant or of less importance than the "big" things, like holding some high office or making a million dollars? The common experience is that most of our activities in this life are things we all would classify as small. Even if we do hold a high office or make a million dollars, our daily lives will be like moving the tiny beads on a rosary. Both the rich and the poor have innumerable little duties and opportunities for loving actions. Life is not a series of big things. It is a parade if tiny possibilities.

Real inner freedom comes when we become what Zen teacher Suzuki Roshi called "nobody special." Think of the people who have been "nobody special" for you! Just doing their work for the honor and not for the glory. Just touching your life with their "little ways." Where would we be without them?

In *Women Who Run With Wolves*, Clarissa Pinkola-Estes wrote, "Ours is not the task of fixing the entire world all at once, but of stretching out to mend the part of the world that is within our reach. Any small, calm thing that one soul can do to help another soul, to assist some portion of this poor suffering world, will help immensely."

It's just fine to shoot for the moon but we may grow more by sharing a Moon Pie and cup of coffee with a homeless person.

Things that Get on My Last Nerve

I am an old bachelor sitting out here all alone in downtown Watering Trough and I have no one but my readers to talk to when things really get on my last nerve. So please, can I just unload some severe irritations on you today?

When I say "downtown Watering Trough" you may be conjuring up visions of a thriving metropolis and see me surrounded by throngs of people, bright lights, dancing in the streets and all the things you find in downtown Chattanooga these days. My friends, downtown Watering Trough is more like downtown Gobbler's Peak. Listen, outhouses only disappeared here in the last decade. You can still see folks hanging their clothes on a line.

Don't get me wrong. I love it here because a train track runs right through it and I love to hear trains late at night. A creek even runs through it and I swam naked in it until I was grown. I still have urges to do that but I don't look near as good without my clothes as I once did. I don't want to shock the cows in Sterchi's pasture.

So if you've now pulled up on your mental screen a picture of a lonely old love-starved dude with no one to talk to, you are tuned into the light channel.

Sometimes I think I will bust if I can't tell some-one how disgusted I am with certain things Like skinny people who can eat all they want and never gain a pound. Sometimes County Auditor Bill McGriff takes me to lunch and while I eat small portions of lean beef, cottage cheese, and green beans to keep my stomach from obstructing my view of home plate, that Sand Mountain bone yard eats enough for the Big Orange football team and never gains an ounce. Some times I turn him down when he invites me to lunch because I have days when my self-control is running low and I have the feeling I might slap him upside the head with a wet squirrel if I have to look at that lean frame one more time.

Claude Ramsey used to disgust me that way. You could read a newspaper through him. I could hardly stand to be around the man. These days I like him a lot. He has filled out real well. I think having a decent job with a big salary has been good for him.

If they ever expand the coverage of our capital punishment laws, I want people who never gain a pound added to the list. If anyone deserves the needle, they do. Since there are more of us than there are of them, I believe we finally have the political clout to get them out of our face.

Don't get me started on these morons who talk about schools and say, "You can't solve the problem with money." Doesn't money buy buildings, teachers, books, computers, blackboards and chalk? I am not suggesting we put the needle to them. That would be too merciful. We just need to put them in a room and when they ask for food, say, "Money will not solve your problem."

Another person who deserves the needle is the one who invented that little price strip scotch-taped on top of CDs. Every time I open a new CD I pause and hate him. Sometimes I have to walk around the block before I can settle down enough to finish opening the thing. I tear a little piece off and try to flip it in the waste can and it stays stuck to my finger. I then try to unstick it from my finger with the other hand and it sticks to that hand Some of them have a tab saying, "open here." Don't waste your time pulling it. I think the inventor of the strip worked for a drug company specializing in blood pressure pills.

Thanks for listening. I feel better.

See Your Life as a Novel

Esteemed photographer Jack Spencer says, "I honestly believe that a great novel could be written about each and every one of us,"

He should know_ His pictures of old Mississippi musicians and ordinary working people set loose streams of thought that could well make up chapters in novels about each of them, Just think of some powerful pictures you have seen and how vividly they spoke about the persons and you will know what I mean.

He adds, "We all have wondrous tales written across our faces. Some are epic, some tragic, some hilarious, some elegiac ...but none would be uninteresting."

I rarely read novels but after reading a review of "Circle of Grace" by Penelope Stokes, I had to know the story. It is a tale of four women who leave college as close friends and pledge to keep in touch via a circle journal they continually pass among them.

What struck me was the intriguing level of drama in each life. It makes you wish there was a complete novel or biography on each of them.

About the time I read Spencer's words I had been sorting out on a table pictures from different decades of my life as well as pictures of my children. I had for-gotten how much action there has been in my life. We get so numbed by the mundane mortar of our days that we fail to back off and see the art show we have hung on the wall of our individual life.

One of my dearest friends is severely retarded. You might wonder what kind of novel could be written about a person with those limitations. He endured almost two years of neglect and physical abuse so severe that it either caused or contributed to his retardation.

In the next chapter he is rescued by a loving woman who wanted him and nurtured him in every possible way. His life turns out to be an exciting saga of adventure and achievement against incredible odds.

Yes indeed, a great novel could be written about each person. If you don't believe it, it may be that you are not paying attention to the unfolding of your own life. It is literally unfolding like the pages of a novel and you have not allowed it to captivate you.

It may be that feelings of unworthiness keep you from seeing the worth of seeing your life in a novel. We all have been baptized repeatedly face forward in the poison waters of unworthiness. It's a wonder we haven't been dissolved like an Alka Seltzer. But wouldn't each of those baptisms make a gripping and exciting chapter in a novel of your life?

If you keep a daily journal, you know how true it is that a novel could be written about each and every one of us. I can spend a single day reading through my journal and see pain and pleasure, defeat and victory, love and despair, vindictiveness and vindication and everything one could ever read in any novel.

A dear friend recently complained to me that she was often depressed over the drabness of her life. I could tell from her email that she is an excellent writer with a fantastic ability to paint word pictures and make boring details come alive. I suggested she write about her own life and share it with her family. She has shared some of those writings with me and I am certain her grandchildren will be laughing and crying over her words a half century from now.

I am not telling you that your life is any more special than the lives of others. What I am telling you is that your life is special. I am telling you your life is as special as the life of any other person who has ever lived. Honor it.

It may never be written up in the chapters of a novel so write it up in the pages of your mind.

Frying Pan and Fire are the Same

People say, –don't jump out of the frying pan into the fire." I say there is no difference. You are completely miserable in either.

That old saying is an impediment to intelligent decision-making. It makes people stay in unhappy situations. They are frozen in place, afraid they will make a mistake.

If you are unhappy where you are (frying pan), what do you have to lose by making a decision to do something else? Is the fire really worse than the frying pan? If you get out of the frying pan, you might end up better off. You might be able to move beyond both the frying pan and the fire.

In my journal one year I made two points about this. I was in a frying pan (unhappy job) and struggling with a decision to change, fearing I might be unhappier.

I wrote, "One kind of unhappiness is no different than another." There may be tiny gradations of unhappiness but basically unhappiness is unhappiness. One kind is so like another that you can hardly tell the difference.

As my sister says, "I wouldn't stretch my fanny for the difference." She tells about three hens. One was a White Leghorn who bragged, "I lay big beautiful white eggs and Farmer Brown gets a dollar a dozen for them." The Rhode

Island Red boasted, "I lay big, lovely brown eggs and Farmer Brown gets ninety cents a dozen for them." A little Bandy hen said, "I lay little eggs and Farmer Brown gets fifty cents a dozen for them but I wouldn't stretch my fanny for the difference."

That's the way I feel about unhappiness. It's all unhappiness. I wouldn't stretch my fanny for the difference.

The second point I wrote in my journal was, "You cannot be happy on any job that provides too few creative outlets for you."

The emphasis here is on the words "for you." We all have creative abilities that are uniquely our own. If your job doesn't allow you to express some of those special talents of your own, you cannot be happy in it. You might use your creativity to mark time as painlessly as possible and to make the best of the situation but you will not really be happy.

These points also apply to relationships. If you are unhappy, think of how little you have to lose by changing things. Once you see clearly that the relationship is making you unhappy and is unlikely to change, it is always time for you to move on. There may be many complicating factors but when you are unhappy, you cannot make anyone else happy and your pie is a mud pie no matter how you cut it.

Your first and only complete responsibility in this life is to yourself. If you do not take care of that #1 responsibility, you will do very little of value for anyone else.

It is not selfish for you to make your happiness your first order of business. In fact, it is selfish for you to be miserable because when yon choose misery, you thereby decide to distribute your unhappiness to everyone in your family and circle of friends. That's as selfish as it gets.

Go Directly to the Dance Floor

A reader wrote in 2003, "Your article defines the new me After a year and a half of cancer treatments, when the music begins I go directly to the dance floor."

Too often those who love to dance will hold back and wait to see if others get up to dance. They will wait for someone to ask them to dance. My reader had always loved to dance but it took a bout with cancer to teach her that now is the time to enjoy what she loves.

If you have been wanting to sing, go directly to a store and buy a sing-a-long outfit with a few good sing-a-along tracks. Don't wait for someone to call you up. Sing! Immediately!

One day at a jam session a man with a great voice sang a couple of songs. I loved his voice and his style and told him he should be singing. He said he couldn't play an instrument. I said, "You have the greatest musical instrument ever made and it was made by God himself. The human voice."

I told him about the sweet pleasure of going to nursing homes and singing for people whose lives are very limited and restricted and urged him to try it. He did buy a boom box and a lot of singalong tapes and began to sing for people. His fever grew until he even made a couple of great CDs.

Most people don't go directly to their dream. A dream is strictly a mental thing, a fantasy of the mind, until you take that first step toward doing it. Go directly to that first step. Don't allow fear to slam you to the mat and pin you. Just go right to it. Fear cannot survive when hearts, hands and legs are in motion.

I had always dreamed of writing. An advisor said, "Write something within 24 hours and send it to someone." I wrote a letter to the editor on an issue I understood. Imagine my delight when the editor put a big border around it and featured it on the op-ed page! One of my supervisors called me in and asked,

"Where have you been hiding, boy?" Within weeks he doubled my salary. All because I went straight to the dance floor.

No matter what you want to do, you must break the lethargy of plain old laziness and do something. Go directly to the dance floor. Don't wait for cancer to remind you that your days here are limited to do what your heart desires. You may have to start small (what's smaller than a letter to the editor?) but remember that Jesus said when we are faithful over little things we will be given bigger things.

I have quit worrying about how big the successes are that come to me. It is enough to just be doing what I love. As long as there's a bean on the table and my hands are on the computer keys or the neck of my guitar. I am happy and floating in the blue skies of life.

If you had taught Chet Atkins his first chord on a guitar and died a month later, you might have died thinking you had never accomplished anything with your music, not knowing that young boy from Luttrell, Tennessee would go on to be one of the world's greatest guitarists.

It is not our place to decide what is big and what is

little. We don't have a set of eternal scales. We are so hypnotized by the crazy, sick values of society and its inherent phoniness that we cannot conceive the worth of anything. If we do our work with care and a loving heart, that is enough, that is very big.

Do one thing today for your heart's deepest desire. Look upon it as your love affair with God. Go directly to the dance floor.

Bite-size Pieces of Perfection

A friend sent me an email saying, wish you little bite-size pieces of perfection that give you the funny feeling someone is smiling on you."

That phrase, "little bite-size pieces of perfection" stuck with me. I look for them and I think I am getting better at it. It has improved the quality of my days.

In my journal I often write up those little bite-size pieces of perfection to hone my appreciation and observation skills. Start zeroing in on your juicy, delicious moments and you will get a big surprise: they will come more often!

That which we mull over multiplies in our lives. Job said, "That which I feared has come upon me." There is a psychological/spiritual law operating here and I once heard it described as Job's Law. That law declares that we magnetize substance and energy with our attention. Fear will magnetically draw fearful thoughts and experiences into our lives.

Thank God there is an opposite law activated by gratitude and appreciation. I call it the Loaves and Fishes Law. Right before He multiplied a few fish and pieces of bread, Jesus prayed a prayer of gratitude. Metaphysically viewing the Bible, the message of that story is that gratitude is a multiplying energy.

Your bite-size pieces do not have to be something spectacular to others. It is only important that they be spectacular to you.

An experience I had this morning illustrates this truth. For over a decade I have had a Saturday break-fast with a songwriter who writes for my music publishing company. Most days he will complain over something, most often over the crispness of the bacon or whether his eggs are cooked "over medium well." Today they didn't fulfill his order to his satisfaction but he smiled and told the apologetic waitress, "Oh that's alright. I will be just fine." I viewed this as a major spiritual development in his life and it was spectacular to me.

Normally I am not into this whole concept of perfection because I have seen too many lives spoiled by addiction to perfection. Long ago I clearly saw it is much healthier to just learn to be a better human.

Anyway, perfection is a highly subjective thing, meant to be savored in small doses. Watching for them can become your favorite game each day. Days you find more than one are grand-slam home-run days.

Recently I was sitting in my car on a warm spring day talking with a friend. A pretty butterfly flew in. I stopped and told her about a butterfly spending the day with me one day when I was working in my garden, lighting on my hat, and then on my arm sipping the apple cider I placed there for her. I said, "Let me see if this one will be friendly and get on my finger." I held out my finger and she climbed right on it. She sat there during the rest of our conversation though the car windows were both down. When I drove home she stayed in the car.

Near the Tennessee Aquarium there are lots of flowers and the Tennessee River flowing nearby. I had tried to shoo out her out while driving home but she wanted to stay. When I stopped for a traffic light at the Aquarium, I rolled down the window and said, "Here's you a paradise with flowers and water. I've enjoyed you but for your own pleasure, I think you should get out here." I lowered the window and she immediately flew away.

It matters not that people look at me with that little cynical smile when I tell them about my experiences with other species. I am not trying to amass a body of believers. I am just enjoying every little bite-size piece of perfection that comes my way.

Make it a habit and it will keep you happy.

I Wish I Had Hugged Minnie Pearl

In June of 2003 I retained in my daily journal a copy of a letter I wrote to Bill Littleton. Let me just go straight to that letter:

> When I was writing at Cedarwood Music in the early 70s, Minnie Pearl would come by the front desk and chat with her friend Dolly Denny. They would chatter and gossip and giggle like two schoolgirls. I was awed by her child-like nature and overwhelming pleasantness.
>
> While I was dying to meet her, I never could bring myself to interrupt her wonderful laugh sessions with Dolly. But one day when I came in Dolly stopped me and introduced me to Minnie. I wanted to hug her so bad. I wish now I had.

This experience of disappointment in myself taught me the valuable lesson to maximize the spiritual juice I get out of the people in my life.

You see, that's what I wanted from Minnie Spiritual juice. You could get a super charge of it just looking into her face. That was part of her power and glory. When she and Dolly had their get-togethers, you could feel an electric aura spread through the entire office. I know you know exactly what I am talking about be-cause we have all known people who were bigger than life. As the Psalmist said, "Their cups run over."

I am certain I would have gotten that hug from Minnie if I had just asked for it. She was always hugging people and letting her sweet inner self permeate their being.

When I was a boy I would walk across the railroad tracks behind our home place and go down to Chickamauga Creek to fish. Sterchi's Dairy always had a big patch of sugar cane in that area which they ground up for their dairy silo. I would take my pocket knife and cut off a stalk, then cut it into six inch pieces, then split the hard outer covering and take out the sweet pith. When I'd bite into it, juice would literally squirt out. In my memory, few things stand out as that delicious.

Look at the people in your life and you will immediately know those with the greatest spiritual juice. Seek ways to be with them. Ask them for a hug. They are your spiritual transformers.

I have few regrets in my life but two of them are that I didn't go to Missouri and visit my favorite poet and writer, James Billet Freeman, and then to Texas to meet Hall of Fame songwriter Floyd Tollman. From afar, they constantly pumped their creative juice into my spiritual carburetor. I did correspond with Freeman for 11 years and a close friend of Tollman's often sent me notes and photos about his life and shared some stories that made me feel I actually knew him.

Fortunately, we don't have to drive halfway across the country to find people who resonate powerfully with our own souls. They are all around us and most of them are pleased to share their essences with us.

I went to Nashville a few years ago and spent a day

with Bill Littleton to get juiced up. No one writes about music and the creative self with more juice than Bill. If you are a writer or artist of any kind or if music is one of your passions, you may want a trial subscription to his newsletter *The Bridgeworks*.

Yes, I wish I had hugged Minnie Pearl. But it's OK. I have hugged her many times in my heart.

We are a Bad Influence on Hummingbirds

Timmy was a little hummingbird who came to my feeder every summer for years. This year he didn't show up and I finally asked Lulu about him. Lulu was his faithful wife of many years. No telling how many eggs she had laid for Timmy.

As she sat on my finger, tears dropped off her tiny face as she began to speak. "Timmy fell in the gulf last fall, I am sad to say. He just didn't have the fat for the return trip."

I asked, "What's fat got to do with it?" and she said, "Oh, the fat we build up just before flying south is our fuel for that long first leg of the journey to Cuba. You had better have a nice little belly when you head out or you will not make it."

"Why didn't he have the fat?" I asked.

"Well, he had a fine belly going until two transients discovered your feeder. He fought them off from sunup until sundown every day. All the time I was begging him to stop but he seemed to become more macho every day. He kept saying 'There's not enough to go around!'"

"Such a waste of life!" I said with great sadness. "Didn't he know I had plenty for all?"

She said, "I peeped in your window one day and saw you had a knob you could twist and enough water came out to fill our feeder for years. I told Timmy and he said there wasn't enough sugar and all that water would do us no good without sugar. He said, 'Those two little Yankee hoboes from Michigan are not going to slurp up our good southern water and I mean it. Now stop nagging me about fighting them off!'"

"What pointless behavior," I exclaimed, "I had a huge canister of sugar there in the kitchen."

"Timmy wouldn't have believed it," she said, then hung her little head and sobbed. If you've never seen a hummingbird sob you may never know the meaning of true grief.

I asked her to tell me about his last moments and she said, "He flew alright for a while then I saw him losing altitude. I flew up beside him and asked what was wrong. He said he was getting tired and just want-ed to give up. I begged him to keep trying. I thought I would die when he made the final plunge_ When he hit the water he didn't even make a splash. There's something heartbreaking about living a long life and then not even making a little splash at the end."

I asked if she'd found a new mate. She said, "Yes, he's a lot younger but it looks like he is no different than Timmy. I told him what happened to Timmy and yet he is still fighting every bird that comes near your feeder. Here we are close to time for the long flight south and he has wasted most of his belly in hostile behavior.'

Suddenly I started feeling superior to hummingbirds and said, 'lulu, how could Timmy be so stupid? Fighting like a maniac over nothing! When will you hummingbirds conquer these insecurities and fears that make you lash out at each other?"

Lulu looked perplexed. "You really don't know, do

you?"

"Know what?" I asked.

"That all of us have become what we are by watching humans. You've been killing each other all along. Sometimes over a dollar and oftentimes over things that are downright ridiculous Timmy was just as smart as you, Mr. Roberts."

Miffed. I went inside and read the paper. Sure enough there was a story about people fighting over water out in the west. On every page there were killings, rapes, robberies and every kind of insane conduct you can imagine. And, of course, another crazy war.

I went back outside and apologized to Lulu. I sure am glad she can't read.

In Search of a Real Tomato

If there is anything better than a tomato sandwich on white bread, smeared liberally with mayonnaise, the good Lord must have kept it for the angels in heaven. One thing is for sure - they transport me to heaven.

I remember one time when they saved my life. We were providing music in a rural church for a week and staying with a farm family there. The first morning we awoke with chickens roosting on the foot of the bed (I kid you not). At breakfast there was a big trough against the dining room wall where they fed scraps to the dogs, cats and house chickens. It was liberally covered with green flies. The man of the house told us, "Me and the missus have caught stomach amoebas and we can't figger how it happened." Suddenly we all got nauseous and after breakfast went into town and got a big basket of tomatoes, two big loaves of white bread and a large jar of mayonnaise. That's all we ate for days, fleeing the attack of the stomach amoebas.

I was beginning to think I would not get to enjoy one this year. My efforts to get the right tomatoes kept meeting with defeat.

When it comes to what we southerners call "mater sandwiches," it is easy to wander into sin. The first sin is to use anything but white bread. If you ever do that, go somewhere and hide your face for several days and beg your taste buds for forgiveness

The second potential sin is to not use enough mayonnaise. If you are dieting, it is better to just abstain from one of these heavenly delights than to not use mayonnaise or to use too little.

A third sin is to tell someone a tomato is "a Dayton Mountain tomato" when it is merely driven near Dayton Mountain. That sin was committed against me twice this summer. The first time I was in the metropolis of downtown Dayton to dine at Dayton Café with my pal, "Barnacle" Morgan, and there on the courthouse square I saw the first tomatoes of the season.

I ran over there and asked, "Are those really Dayton Mountain tomatoes?" and the lady said, "Yes, sir, I picked 'ern this morning." I bought a bag and they were nothing but hard, red softballs. You would have needed to pour a half bottle of catsup on one to get the slightest tomato taste.

You see Dayton Mountain is to tomatoes as Vidalia is to onions. At least it always had been for me until this first contact with a homegrown tomato in 2004. I am convinced that sweet lady was really from Chicago and came all the way down here to find a dumb hill-billy. She succeeded.

Shortly thereafter I was visiting my sister and she said, "Would you like a tomato sandwich made with a Dayton Mountain tomato?" After a short swoon, I panted, "Oh, yes...please make me one." As soon as I saw her take out that hard red softball, I knew the Chicago lady had found her second hillbilly of the season.

What is going on with tomato farmers? Those big red hard tomatoes were invented to make us miss real tomatoes during the winter months. Just to evoke memories of tomatoes in the minds of gullible simple-tons like me.

They were created for shipping. I am certain it was a good moneymaking idea. I have no doubt you could ship one to Russia via Mexico, South America, and Australia with the last two hundred miles of the journey being by Siberian sled delivery and it would still be as "fresh" as the day it was shipped. And as tasteless.

The wondrous news is that a friend from Fiery Gizzard dropped me off a real tomato and I just finished dining in succulent splendor. I can face the bitter winter now. I have had my mater sandwich.

The Universe Honors Tomato Thoughts

A good neighbor will tomato you, using "tomato" here as a verb meaning, "come to your rescue when you are tomato-less and make certain you have an adequate supply of tomatoes for an entire summer of tomato sandwiches."

Last summer I didn't plant a garden for the first time in 25 years and I wrote a column about my desperate search for good-tasting tomatoes. I was so irritable and hateful all summer that my good neighbors must have noticed. One day this past April my neighbor, Wayman Wilson, showed up with a shovel and four Better Boy tomato plants. He said, "I read about you not gardening due to stooping problems and I want you to at least have some tomatoes for those sandwiches you missed out on last year. Where do you want them planted?" I have an old metal swing structure where I haye always tied plants so I told him to plant them underneath it.

As much as I like Better Boys, I have always want-ed to try Brandywines. I noticed in Organic Gardening that Brandywines usually win their famous tomato tasting contest Shortly after Wayman planted the Better Boys, the pride and joy of Birchwood, Hoyt Branham, showed up one morning and asked, "How would you like to try a Brandywine tomato plant this year?" I grabbed it and stuck it right in the middle of the Better Boys.

Isn't it amazing how the Universe honors our thoughts? I was sending out my desire for great to-matoes and the Universe bounced that right back to Wayman and Hoyt. It sure makes you think more of the Universe and friends like Wayman and Hoyt who tune into it.

Why did I want them under the old swing set structure? I am glad you asked. I am a pantyhose man. Years ago I discovered that pantyhose carry static electricity directly into plants if they are grounded to metal. In a thunderstorm with a lot of static electricity, you can stand there and watch them grow. I'm a politician and I wouldn't lie to you.

My shallow Americans, I want you to know that I have never been so tomatoed in my life. I have been eating them with everything. Sara Lee has had to add an extra shift since I discovered their white bread makes the best sandwiches. Kraft is working their Miracle Whip assembly line overtime.

Yes, I prefer Miracle Whip with my tomato sand-wiches. I am just now coming out of the closet. I know the abuse you mayo purists are going to inflict upon me but I will feel unfaithful to Miracle Whip if I don't just admit my preference.

A tomato sandwich lover wrote a letter to the editor telling me the proper name for one is a "sink sandwich" - one you need to stand over the sink to eat. She referred me to the White Trash Cookbook and sure enough, it is called that in this treasure chest of recipes from Ten Speed Press (www.tenspeedpress.com). I find it works well for me to just sit on a beach towel on the floor. Daintiness has never been a major objective for me.

A sweet young thing from Lookout Valley visited

my domicile last week and she said, "Your face is red!" and I replied, "Yes! Want a tomato sandwich?" I do believe I can snag more women with tomato sandwiches than with Lee Anderson's Corvette. After a fresh tomato sandwich, a woman purrs like a kitten and simply cannot keep her hands off you.

The strangest thing about this year's tomato crop

is that Wayman planted them in old hard dirt that has never been fertilized and worked. There are four Brandywines hanging there that are somewhere between softball and volleyball size (remember, I wouldn't lie to you) and still green. They will be basketballs soon.

Pray they don't all ripen at the same time for I might hurt myself.

Savor Each Bite of Life

The only thing better than tasting everything you have ever wanted is to truly taste one thing. If you have not learned to truly taste one thing, it would be a superficial experience to taste everything.

There is a good story in one of Thich Nhat Thanh's books. His family was very poor but when his mother went to the market she always brought home one of his favorite cookies. He would sit and smell the cookie before taking that first bite. He would wait a long time between bites. It was the only cookie he would have for days and he wanted to totally savor it.

I did not have an all-day cookie when I was a child but I did have an all-day sucker. The end of that thing looked like a tennis ball. To this day I can still taste those things.

We found a trick to extend the pleasure of our bubble gum. When the flavor would wear thin from hours of chewing, we'd roll it in sugar or sprinkle a little cinnamon on it and go at it one more time.

One day I walked in on my father and he was eating Eagle Brand milk out of the can. I had never seen him do it before and asked him about it. He told me he was the oldest of eleven children in his family and had to help raise all his brothers and sisters. His twin sisters were not strong and the doctor told them to make

their bottle formula with Eagle Brand. Dad loved the smell of it and sneaked an occasional tiny taste but the family was too poor for him to have all he wanted. He said, "I decided if I ever got grown and made enough money I would eat all the Eagle Brand milk I wanted." Sure enough, there he was eating spoonfuls of it.

How thoughtlessly we speed through many of our meals. We get much less of the nutrition from them than we would if we went slow and really relished every bite.

Wolfing down food forces the stomach to do what the teeth are designed to do. It must often pass poorly chewed food on down the line and the body ends up getting little benefit from it.

Brownie was my favorite childhood dog but he never was healthy because he would not eat anything but wieners. No matter how big you cut the pieces, he swallowed them whole. We tried the fanciest dog foods on him but he was strictly a wiener dog.

At the end of WWII when one of the concentration camps was liberated by allied troops, one of the in-mates was clearly healthier than all the others. He ex-plained his secret. He said he chewed every bite of his food and chased it with nothing but a tiny sip of water. The enzymes in his saliva assured maximum nutrition from his pitiful diet. By not diluting the food in his stomach with a lot of liquid, he got the full advantage of complete digestion.

Purely aside from the nutritional advantages of slow chewing and minimal liquids, there are definitely health advantages to savoring each bite. Deepak Chopra, renowned Ayurvedic physician, says we should taste a little of everything on the table. He says taste buds are directly connected to different areas of the brain and food enjoyment keeps those brain areas alive and vigorous. So we should eat slow and pleasurably for our brain's sake.

How much difference would it make in our happiness if we lived each day in a "cookie" frame of mind9 I have found a trick that helps me to do this. When I find myself truly enjoying something, whether it is food or fellowship with a friend, I simply say to my monkey mind, "Freeze!" Then I consciously slow down and take in the experience with all my awareness.

Try it. Remember you have taste buds in your soul, too.

Life is Like a Guitar

Naman Crowe sent me an email saying, "Life can be like a guitar. We''all get out of tune at times, even pop a string now and then."

What an interesting way to look at life! I know from experience it is true. Once when I was in a down time I asked my mother for help and she said, "Son, what's the first thing you do when you pick up your

guitar?" I told her I checked to see if it was in tune and she said, "I know. And if you'll allow the Lord to tune you up, you will overcome this problem you now face."

Thinking of a guitar, I see the bottom E-string is the smallest but it stands for excitement and that is not a small matter in our lives. Most guitarists tune all the other strings by the bottom E. So we need to keep our excitement each day to stay in tune.

You say, "Oh, you don't know what a drag my job is or you would know I cannot possibly be excited in the morning when I go to work." Yes I do know perfectly well how you feel because I have had jobs that made me search them for something exciting. The

harder it is to find something exciting about a job, the more important it is to keep searching until you find it. We will find one exciting task or at least one exciting person there if we will simply set aside our totally negative mindset and look for it.

The second string (B) stands for bravery. You don't need to have Medal of Honor bravery. You only need enough for the day. Thank goodness we only have to live one day at a time. There are times when it is not easy to find even one of the millions of good reasons to live but we can swing it for one tiny day.

The third string (G) stands for gratitude. How many times when we get persimmon-mouthed do we sweeten our attitude by remembering all the reasons we have to be grateful?

The fourth string (D) stands for daring. Those who succeed often point back to the time they dared to take one risk. The most important judgment we make is knowing the difference between daring and recklessness. The daring look at all the risks before leaping and the reckless just leap.

The fifth string (A) stands for appreciation. There is a difference between gratitude and appreciation. Gratitude comes from the inner grin of counting blessings and appreciation comes from the spiritual exercise of weighing value. How rich our, life becomes when we cultivate the habit of weighing the worth of people and events.

The sixth string (E again) stands for endurance. There is a short verse in Ephesians that simply says, "Having done all, stand." Everyone faces tunnels, long stretches of bad roads through barren deserts and times of blinding rain. Yes, there are times we get through by simply enduring, putting one foot in front of the other. These are times when we break a string on the guitar of life and cannot make music until we are able to replace and retune it.

Even the cheapest guitars can become dear to you. I learned to play on a warped old Stella. I am now having an identical old Stella restored just for old times sake. Don't block out of your memory the hard years of your life. You were learning something needed for your ultimate success.

Remember, too that even one out-of-tune string makes the whole guitar sound out of tune. Keep balance. Check each string often.

Once we get in tune, we have this need to be with others who are in tune and make some music. That's why we are always looking around for a good jam session. If you find one, be sure and call me.

Giving Advice is Fun

I once wrote a column advising you against giving advice. The main reason I gave was that no one takes it. In a half century of giving advice no one had ever taken mine Nor had they taken the advice of others I have known with vastly superior intellects.

At the time I wrote that column I had ceased giving advice to anyone at any time. Pretty soon I started noticing how unhappy I was becoming I asked old Doc Findley to prescribe some smiley pills for me and he said, "Let us first see if we can find the root of your existential emptiness (Tennessee Temple grads use big words like that). How long has it been since you gave someone a little advice?"

"Oh Doc, I quit giving advice long ago when I noticed that no one really wants it," I said with a feeling of superiority.

"Aha!" he yelped, "right there is your problem. You have been stifling a human drive as strong as the need for food, water, or sex." He took out his prescription pad and wrote, "Give someone advice today."

I was stunned. I thought Doc was losing his mind again. But I love him so much I decided to honor his prescription. As soon as I stepped out on the street,

I saw a man with a furrowed brow. I said, "Sir, per-chance do you have a problem tody," and he began to tell me how bad his wife was treating him.

How lucky he was! If there's anything I am full of advice about its wives. I unloaded my wagon on this poor sucker and by the time I walked to my car, my existential emptiness had disappeared. Like David of old I felt so good I wanted to run through a troop and leap over a wall. Driving home I kept murmuring to myself, "Doc is a genius."

So please forget that I once counseled you not to counsel. If you repress your counseling drive, you are headed straight into existential emptiness.

In the first place, any fool who has no better sense than to ask you for advice deserves it. Have no mercy. Cut him no slack. Never concern yourself that he will not follow it. It is not important that he accept your advice. It only matters that you give it. When you carry around a headful of wisdom, it gets heavy to tote. Get it out, my friend. If you don't you're going to be asking your doctor for smileys. Do not spend the rest of your life walking around with that pasted-on smiley grin.

You may be wrestling with the guilty thought that it cannot be right to do something simply because it makes you feel good. Look at it this way: we all know no one really wants or acts on our good advice. So giving it to them doesn't hurt them at all. There's an old Huna teaching that the only sin is to intentionally hurt another human being. Since there is no danger they will take your advice, you cannot hurt them. It's too beautiful for words!

Notice the warm feeling that steals over you when you give advice. It tastes and feels like warm honey. It is the closest you will ever come to omniscience and omnipotence. The closest thing to reality is feeling. Even though you may not really be all knowing and all-powerful, just feeling that way for even a nana-second is priceless.

I went to a restaurant and their corn sticks almost broke my teeth. I sent them this advice: You are missing a lot of money by not marketing your corn sticks to the military. They would be lethal in hand to-hand-combat. You could also market them to railroads for use as spikes. They are just as strong as metal spikes and cheaper to make.

How sweet it is to counsel. Never miss a chance.

A New Look at Net Worth

My old city government cohort Don Bain got me to thinking about our use of the term "net worth." He asked, "Should a person's net worth be expressed in dollars and cents, or should it be expressed in other terms?"

He goes on, "We've all known people who have been poor and had to struggle to get by, but they may have had a heart of gold."

It seems to me that he has answered his own question. The gold in your heart is as valuable as the gold in your bank account. Who would you rather be around, rich people with no goodness in their hearts or a dear friend with a heart of gold?

Let's face it. Some of us don't know how to make money because we have never given it the time and priority required. Making money does require a setting of one's mental sails. So do the other intangibles we could list as a part of our net worth. Things like character, integrity, friendliness, a sense of humor and a sense of wonder.

Maybe I would list a sense of wonder as the top value in one's net worth. My father told me a story that makes the point vividly. He took mother to a beach one night and she walked off to be alone a few minutes. When he joined her she was standing under a banyan tree and the ocean spray was coursing down her face along with her own tears. She was so moved she could hardly speak and when she did she said, "Roy, the Great Spirit is here."

That is one of my family "story mandalas" I fall back on when I need a boost. A mental picture of my father and mother standing by the ocean with tears streaming down their faces, in awe of God's creation.

It's things like this -- common occurrences in our home -- that never allowed me to be an atheist. God was just too present in the day-to-day happenings in our home. It had to be God because nothing less could give you that melt-the-heart feeling that stabs you through with ecstatic wonder.

Certainly a sense of humor is a vital part of our net worth. Pickle-mouthed people can take you plumb down to the ground. If I were convicted of a capital offense the worse punishment a judge could inflict on

We are Always Going Home

Home is not a house where we grew up. It is a warm place in our heart and we are always going home_

The song "Precious Memories" says "old home scenes of my childhood in fond memory appear." All of the old scenes that we fondly recall are right there in that drawer of our soul marked "home."

The actual house where I spent most of my early years was just a part of the warm place evoked by the word "home." One tiny little wall plaque with a picture of a Robin and a Sparrow has meant more to me over the years than the physical structure. It read:

Said the Robin to the Sparrow I would really like to know

Why these anxious human beings Rush about and worry so

Said the Sparrow to the Robin Friend, I think that it could be They have no heavenly father Such as cares for you and me

I cannot speak the word home without thinking of that plaque. It created a warm place in my heart that will always be calling me home.

We had a huge oak tree in the front yard we called "Oakie" and talked about it like it was cherished member of the family. Indeed, it was. We hung a swing from it and it provided many hours of delirious fun to us in our "swinging years. "Not long ago I went by and took one of Oakie's leaves home with me as a "point of contact "with home. Have you ever pressed down in your journal a leaf from a tree or a place you love? It has magical powers to take you back home.

My sister painted me a snow scene of a crooked tree in the back of our yard. It curved out like it was designed to be a seat and extended over a branch where water often gurgled along. I was forty years old before I read a book about meditation but one of the places

I meditated without knowing the word or its meaning was sitting on that tree limb. I treasured my sister's painting of it and someone took it from my office 20 years ago. It was a piece of home I lost and I am hoping she will paint it again.

Home is more than a place. It is people you learned to love, people you walked with through both joyous and wrenching times. The father of a family living next door to us in my earliest years died, leaving a widow and four children. The men in the community built them a house on our property. Lelia Mae and Tiny were my age and we grew up together. Every time I see them, I go home again. People you love can immediately transport you back home.

Home can be some little place no one else knows about. Wiley "Goose" Adams and I took a pick and shovel down to Chickamauga Creek. We dug out a secret room in a high bank of the creek covered by tree branches. We would pull back the limbs, climb back in our room, and catch fish all day long. No one else in the world ever knew about our little home away from home. When Goose was dying I gave him a mas-sage one day and talked about things we had done and I know he heard me because he gave me a heavenly going-home smile.

After mother died, Dad told me, "I have not been happy here since your mother went home." It may seem strange to talk of someone going home when they die. It is my deep belief that we have a subconscious inner knowledge that this world is not our original and final home. There is something in us that remembers that home beyond this realm.

Home is little pieces of love stored in our heart by people and places. Is it any wonder that we are always going home?

Birds Teach Parenting Lessons

My computer window is a porthole on the world. Lately I have been watching birds raise their offspring and I think they are better parents than humans.

They know the power of repetition. I saw a purple finch teaching a baby to pick up and crack a sunflower seed. He would fly to the feeder and wait for the baby to fly to his side. He would slowly take out a seed and turn his head toward the baby and say, "Watch, Buster, and I will show you how." Then he would crack it and eat it while junior sat there with his mouth open. After he ate two or three he would feed junior one, then leave him alone on the feeder. When the little dummy didn't crack one on his own, Papa just repeated the lesson

Repetition tires humans but most children only learn a lesson after it is repeated 327 times. That's not laboratory research. It is strictly based on the number of times it took me to learn something my father or mother tried to tell me. There's a little automatic turnoff valve in the heads of kids that closes whenever a parent says, "Now listen to me! This is important." Keep on. On the 328th time, they will have it.

Papa Purple taught his son self-effort. He didn't robotically buy him a car on his 16th birthday with no effort on his part. He would crack a sunflower seed and hold it in his beak so sonny boy could see it, then swiftly fly off to a limb and wait for him to come and get a bite.

An hour went by without junior cracking his first seed. He left him on the feeder and disappeared in a tree. Baby Purple looked frantic and abandoned. After a few minutes of aloneness, hunger hit him. He went back to the seeds. When he finally cracked one, he looked shocked. While I applauded, his patient father zoomed in from the tree where he was hiding to express his pride.

Bluebirds are great parents. While they are egg sitting or the babies are small, they will try to drive off any predator. Those in my box have driven off a cat, a blue jay and a nosy starling this year. One year they ejected crows! It was a hilarious sight to see a tiny bluebird chase two big crows across my back yard and over the treetops far away.

They didn't drown their babies in the bathtub or put them in a car and run them into a lake or shake them until their brains were damaged Thank God blue-birds don't take child-rearing lessons from humans. A bluebird once told me, "If humans are God's greatest handiwork, we are all in deep trouble."

Bluebirds are also good at arousing the curiosity of their babies and making them see the world's great possibilities. When the babies are tiny, they enter the box to take them food. The babies think their little box is the whole world. As the babies get to the pre-flight stage, they hold the food just inside the box, forcing them to come and get it, knowing it will give them a peek at this big old world. Then they actually hold it just outside so the babies will have to stick their heads out the door.

Bluebirds have read that verse in the Old Testament about God motivating us to action "as an eagle stirreth her nest." Eagle nests are made of sharp sticks. When eagle parents get ready for their young to get out of the nest and get a job, they stir the sticks so sharp points will create too much discomfort for them to remain at home. They say, "Really, ten years is too long to work on a bachelor's degree. Hit the road, Jack."

Too bad human parents can't take Child Rearing 101 from Professor Bluebird and Dr. Eagle.

Boogie Buck Fell's Last Days

No matter what your work may be, could you carry on with it almost to the moment of your death if you had cancer of the colon and liver? I mean, with no painkillers except the regular OTC pills?

To carry this one step further, could you smile and laugh and make music and make people smile and laugh and be happy right up to the moment of collapsing from the pain?

That's exactly what Boogie Buck Fell did up until he was rushed to St. Thomas Hospital from his gig at Caesar's Restaurant on White Bridge Road in Nashville the second week in January, 2003. Imagine the pain the man experienced the last weeks of his life. He must have been made of steel.

Buck and I had our political differences. He alternated his performing between Memphis, Nashville and Chattanooga and when he lived in Chattanooga he regularly fired off long letters to the editor. He was not classifiable in any way in any part of his being but if he had been politically classifiable, I would describe his politics as extremely irascible independent conservatism with frequent forays into populism and a once-in-a-blue-moon splash of liberalism. He was a Buck Fell indelicancrat.

He was equally outspoken on non-political matters.

He actually got barred from some Internet opinion boards for his rants on music. I particularly agreed with some of his pummelings of contemporary country music, which may be contemporary but is definitely not country under any historical definition of that word. No matter where he stood on any issue, I found his rants to be interesting, sincere-to-the-bone and worth reading. In one paragraph you'd want to choke him and in another you'd want to hug him.

One thing is for sure: when he sat down at the grand piano, you were going to be royally entertained. You were going to laugh and cry. You were going to remember and reminisce. You were going to hear songs you had never heard in your life, a few from today's charts and dozens you hadn't heard in decades, all stirred up in Jerry Lee Lewis rock, Little Richard roll, Frank Sinatra pop, Hank Williams country soul, and gut bucket Delta blues. There was absolutely no end to his repertoire and he had no problem playing any genre of music. You just had to fasten your seat belt and be ready for whatever came out of those long, skinny, miraculous fingers.

He was homeless the last time I saw him, just weeks before his death. Sleeping in his old gasping Cadillac. Getting up every morning and going to the public library to check his email. So how in the world did he own a grand piano?

His old car didn't bother his pride but he wasn't about to play any piano but the best. He tailor-made a trailer rig to haul it around and to protect it from the elements. The night we stood and talked for an hour on the Baymont Motel parking lot he talked about setting up his grand the next day at Caesar's.

I was alone there at the Baymont and had an extra

bed in my room. I offered it to Buck but he said, patting his rusted-at-the-seams Caddie, "No, thanks a bunch but I'll just stay here in my fine mobile home."

I figured he might need a few bucks but knew better than to offer him anything. He had his pride about such things So I asked, "Buckaroo, when you gonna have a CD out?" And he said, "I am working on one right now." I gave him $20 and said, "I would be honored to have the first copy." He grinned and said, "You got it, partner."

Unless someone miraculously discovers some master tapes, I will never have that CD. But I've got Boogie Buck. He will forever pound the ivory keys of my mind.

We Can Have Peace in Insane Times

Recently I let myself lose my peace thinking about the insanity of violence going on in the world. The pain of 9-11 and the way we added to that world pain by attacking a country that had nothing to do with 9-11; the unbelievable hatred that impelled five men to kill all those people in London; a serial rapist who killed a whole family so he could kidnap two small children and use them as sex toys, then killed the young boy and would have killed the young girl when he got through with her.

At times I have thought I might be too sensitive to the pain of this world. But what good is a life where you steel yourself not to feel? How can anyone shut down normal human emotions in one area of life and continue to function with feeling with those they love?

I refuse to shut down my god-given emotional nature. I refuse to become cold and hard. If I am destined to die crying, so be it. I would much prefer that to hardening my heart,

Then I got to thinking about something Jesus said. He was hours away from a fate he knew was coming. He knew he would be unmercifully beaten, cursed and spat upon, then nailed up to slowly die on a crossbeam of wood. Yet he spoke to his dearest friends of peace. He said, "My peace I give to you." How could a man speak of peace at such a time, knowing he would be brutalized?

You may be thinking he used his godhood to close off his fears. I do not think so. He was a feeling man. Remember how he wept when Lazarus died? Remember how Paul said, "He was tempted in all points, like as we"? Remember the verse about him being able

to be touched with the feelings of our infirmities? He loved. He cared. As he was dying he asked John to take care of his grieving mother. He cared and felt his emotions to the end.

His secret is right here: "I do not give peace to you as the world gives." The world can only feel peace when things are peaceful. Jesus tuned into a permanent source of peace. He tuned into peace Itself. He lived in peace and could die in peace. His peace was not dependent on circumstances.

That's the peace he promises us! He said so, "My peace I give to you," We can learn to tune into this deep, unchanging Jesus peace.

In writing a chapter of a autobiography I am starting to work on, I talked about my earliest experiences of God's presence. When I was just a young kindergarten and elementary aged boy, I would go off alone into the deep woods behind our home and listen to God's presence. I didn't say God's voice. I intentionally said "God's presence," because God's presence communicates more clearly than any voice_ What God communicated to me when I was too young to read any sacred book was a deep peace. To this day I can meditate on those experiences and all that deep peace I felt as a small boy returns to me as clear as spring water.

In these days of violence, I am reminding myself of

that peace. The world may not be at peace but we can have peace in this world_ There is a peace dimension of consciousness and Jesus went there hours before his horrible ordeal began and he is able to take you there. He is our Way Shower. People talk of him as "Savior" in reference to a ticket to heaven but for me he has been a savior by showing me the way to live.

When the violence and hatred of insane people starts scribbling furiously on the blackboard of your consciousness, sink yourself completely into the peace of Jesus. He promised it to you and no power on earth can take it from you_

Dancing Can Set You Free

Who in the world would expect one of the great saints to extol the merits of dancing? I receive a daily inspirational quote from the Bruderhof, a spiritual community in Pennsylvania. A recent one was titled "In Praise of Dancing" by St. Augustine.

It came as a large surprise to me but I am happy to be the other pea in a pod with him. It seems to me that people who love to dance are happier than non-dancers.

The venerable saint said, "Dancing demands a freed person, one who vibrates with the equipoise of all his powers." That part about vibrating reminded me of Rocking Raymond, the best rock and roll dancer I have ever seen. For years he came to places where I played and he would smack his feet down so hard it would sound like a clap of thunder.

He became a different person when he hit the dance floor. Years ago I read that Kirlian photography measured the aura of a Swedish woman named Olga Worrell at 16 feet. I believe Rocking Raymond had her beat. He radiated so much energy in all directions that people would gather around the edge of the dance floor to watch him do his thing.

We're not speaking here of some kind of artless, clumsy romping and stomping. No siree. We're talking about something comparable to James Brown. Great coordination and grace of movement. It was a sight to behold.

Another kind of happy dancing is clogging. My favorite clogger is Cindy Pinion, indefatigable promoter of the annual Boxcar Pinion Bluegrass Festival (the great "Boxcar" was her father). You cannot possibly be down in the mouth when you watch Cindy clicking her heels.

One of my harshest critics when I was county executive was Porter Hudlow. Once he was brought before the school board for a hearing to determine whether or not he would continue in his job. The board retired for deliberation of his fate and the roomful of people was surprised when Porter rose and announced, "I don't know about the rest of you folks but I am bored. I think I will dance." He clogged all around the room until the board returned with their decision. After I heard of this I never could dislike Porter again.

I have always been self-conscious about my skill as a rock and roll dancer but for years I took Dr. Bette McGee dancing just for the pleasure of watching her boogie down. She'd put on her feathers and rattles and spangles and set her spirit free. It's one of my favorite memories.

One of my best kept deep, dark secrets is that I sometimes rock and roll when I am home alone. I put on a Delbert McClinton CD and cut up like a new pair of scissors. It's a grand way to get your exercise on a rainy day when you've got the physical blahs and feel like a big sack of sand. St. Augustine said, "I praise the dance for it frees people from the heaviness of matter."

Square dancing is a great way to exercise, lose weight and have fun. Jackie Benderman, my favorite Republican and Primitive Baptist, is living proof of its efficacy. She square dances regularly. It keeps her happy, looking young and beautiful.

Here's the rest of what St. Augustine says about dancing: "I praise the dance for it binds the isolated to community. (It brings) a clear spirit and a buoyant soul. Dance is a transformation of space, of time, of people who are in constant danger of becoming all brain...0 man, learn to dance or else the angels in heaven will not know what to do with you."

If you want your energy field stirred up and cleared of a bunch of old pucker-mouthed inhibitions, tics and spasms, put on some Delbert and get down!

Why Not Live Right Now?

The only time we can live is right now The only place we can be at any time is right where we are If we miss the moment, we are as good as dead.

All the time we are back in the past patting out and playing with the same old mudpies, we are not living. Sandburg was right when he wrote in Prairie, "I tell you the past is a bucket of ashes...a wind gone down."

The past can install a few valuable road signs in our mind but we can easily become one of those John Os-borne said "spend their time mostly looking forward to the past." I saw a bumper sticker that says it all: "Things ain't like they used to be. In fact, they never was."

The future can also take us away from where we are. Jubilee Taylor used to earnestly beseech me to help him get out of his body. I embarked upon serious research to help my precious old pal make an escape. It led me to a Californian named Brother Mulvin. He said buy my book and it will probably get you out of your body; if not, call me and I will talk you out. If this fails, come to see me and for just a hundred dollars I guarantee to get you out. I knew Jubilee wasn't about to spring for a plane ticket to California and another hundred bucks to Brother Mulvin just for a short stroll on the astral cord. Thank goodness he contented himself learning to levitate which isn't all that big a challenge for a drummer.

Our real need is to snuggle down completely in our bodies in the here and now. Doing time travel out in the future, turning flips in what we hope will happen or what we are afraid will happen, is not living.

Living in the now is rare for humans. Everything triggers a memory that drags us back into the past or stirs up a fear that sends us on a dreamy fishing trip into the waters of future time.

If something is so essential to our happiness why is it so hard for us to establish the habit of doing it? One thing that keeps us from being in the present is our habit of judging everything. Someone will occasionally say to me, "I read your columns and agree with most of them." It made me ask myself, "Do I read things just to see if I agree with them or do I read for the experience, stimulation and pleasure? Maybe even to consciously challenge some of the ideas I have melted into old musty, rusty metal molds in my mind?"

Why can't we live each day with the same attitude? Why can't we just sit down and dine at the banquet of this day, this hour, this moment? Why does it need to be a carbon copy of some smudged up old page from our past? Why does it have to be squeezed into tomorrow before tomorrow even peeps over the hill? Why are we allergic to right now?

Emerson said, "We cannot overstate our debt to the past but the moment has the supreme claim." The past was nothing but a birth and a becoming. We made our decisions on the basis of what we knew at that time and the forces that impinged upon us then. As much as we like to talk about what we would do if we had it to do over again, chances are we would do what we did all over again if all we knew was what we knew then.

Elbert Hubbard said, "Remember the weekday to keep it holy." That's a good start. But Rahma Dada Straddlenostrum from downtown Watering Trough says, "Remember this very moment to keep it holy." I believe he read that in the Billy Goat Hill Scrolls.

You May Have Several Callings

Mary Delaney tells about Michaelangelo begrudgingly painting the Sistine Chapel_ He always considered himself a sculptor. We need to get the idea out of our mind that our calling is always something we love to do.

Most of us have multiple callings. How many people do you know who have only one talent? Remembering that Emerson said our callings are our talents, multiple talents mean multiple callings.

My brother Blaine never wanted to be anything but an engineer. My mother used to look at his hands and say, "Oh Blaine, you have the hands of a brain surgeon." I don't think she would have been happy to see him become a proctologist but it didn't matter because he always knew he was going to be an engineer. When he finished the 1 lth grade, he went on to college to set that program in place.

I seldom think about "single calling" people but when I do, I think of Blaine. Engineering is all he's ever done to make a living. But he could have done other things. He's a fine rhythm guitarist. He's a patient nurturer of people. He is a skilled listener - one of the rarest traits on this planet. He would have made an excellent counselor or teacher.

Few people get to do just one thing all their lives.

The Department of Labor years ago said the average American worker will have to re-train seven times during their work years. That's surely a higher number now. It definitely shows that flexibility and adaptability are two requirements of the job market.

We may sometimes gain more acclaim for work that is not our great love. Michaelangelo was more famous for his Sistine Chapel scenes than any of his sculptures.

It will come as a surprise to some but politics was never one of my great loves. My jobs with the city put me in close touch with mayors Olgiati, Kelley and Bender. You would have to be a stone jive idiot to not learn politics sitting under such great politicians. While I didn't love it, I did like it enough to pay attention and I assimilated the masters.

Then I went to the county and observed Chester Frost, Frank Newell, Bob Long, Luke Wilson, Jack Mayfield and other adept politicians. I became good friends with Al Gore, Sr. In the Jaycees I met and liked Bill Brock III. So I was well-baptized by the absolute cream of the crop.

We cannot always do just the work we want to do.

Sometimes circumstances coalesce in such a way that a job lands in our lap to be done. One morning when I was reading a paper and murmuring about the mess in county government at that time, my mother said, "Son, who knows more about that job than anyone?" I answered, "In all honesty, I guess I do." She said, "Well, quit complaining or do something about it." So I ran.

The years I was a Jaycee gave me a taste of the thrill of working for community betterment. I noticed that most of the projects I chaired required the help of one or more elected officials and I remember thinking, "One day I may be able to do a lot more for my hometown by running for office." That's the main reason I ran. If not a single person believed me, I would still say it because it is the truth.

We do get to the point of burn-out quicker with jobs that don't tap into our deepest loves. I became like the near-sighted fox that got romantic with a skunk and said, "Honey, I haven't carried this relationship as far as I would like but I have taken it as far as I can stand."

When you get to that point, do something you love even if you have to live on cornbread and beans. Cornbread and beans taste real good when you're happy.

Freeing Yourself from Grief

Years ago I read a Buddhist story about the importance if taking firm and clear action when someone is taking advantage of us. A young woman told her mother she would meditate every morning and fill her heart full of love and joy but when she went shopping one shopkeeper would subject her to unwelcome caresses. One morning she broke bad and chased the shopkeeper down the road, beating him with her umbrella.

Later she confessed her fit of anger to her teacher and he said, "I remember this whenever someone makes unwelcome advances. Fill your heart with loving-kindness and then with as much mindfulness as you can muster chase him through the streets beating him with your umbrella."

Good people put up with problems longer than they should. It is because they are good, caring, sensitive human beings. They always want to make sure they are doing the right thing. While the person abusing them is not weighed down with such loving considerations, they must move slowly and cautiously lest they hurt someone.

Grungy County coal miner Grady Brewer was a pretty good country philosopher. When someone would come to him and lay out a complicated problem, he would simply say, "If you've got a problem, get rid of it."

Is it always that simple? Maybe not. But often it is

just that simple. All that is needed is clear action to terminate the problem and move on with your life without the person or situation that has become a load too heavy to carry.

One question we can use to determine whether or not the time has come for Grady Brewer-type action is, "How long have I put up with this problem with no change?" The Buddhist lady had put up with the offending shopkeeper much too long. When someone inflicts the same distress on us day after day, it is time to change something. Sometimes the only thing we can change is our tolerance. We absolutely should not accept daily abuse from anyone.

"What if it's your own child?" you might be asking. I repeat, we should not accept daily abuse from anyone. It is unfair to yourself and to the child. It actually teaches the child to abuse you. People learn how to treat us by how we treat our selves. To accept abuse is to teach abuse.

Often such abuse comes from a person who has sworn to love us. A mate who stood hand-in-hand with us and pledged undying love. We need to ask ourselves, "Can someone love me and do these painful things to me all the time?" When it is just an incident and there is an apology, we might accept it. When it becomes a pattern, it's time to implement the Grady Brewer plan.

There are some beautiful Christian, Judaic and Buddhist teachings about turning the other cheek, giving someone your cloak, and responding to violence with kindness. You can do this with people who have a conscience. To respond to their violence with kindness might invoke a twinge of guilt that will lead to a change of heart and behavior. But a serial hurter should not be tolerated. No religion teaches us it is spiritual to be a doormat or a punching bag.

A trusting, kind person may have trouble cranking up the grit and gall to deal with an abusive person or situation. It's good for them to have a tough-minded friend with a low level of fear. I know one woman

who had a friend who was not afraid of her tormenter and she leaned on him until she could get through the transition and free herself of long-term abuse.

We must rid ourselves of the notion that we are being righteous or spiritual in accepting mistreatment. We are denying our God-given dignity. For your sake, stop the cycle before it gets worse. Get your umbrella out and go to work on that hard head.

What I Really Think of Jesus

What I really think of Jesus is that He would not be interested at all in our efforts to make Christmas special by badgering people about saying "Merry Christmas." He would be much more interested in how much our heart feels the sweet meaning of His birth in a stable and being laid in a cattle feeding trough.

He would want to know how much significance that has for us. He would wonder if it caused us to attach more value to being humble and not trying to impress people with how big and powerful we are.

He wouldn't care if the store where we shop has a sign saying "Merry Christmas" or "Happy Holidays." He would be more interested in how much of our time went into shopping for "things" compared to how much time we spent meditating on the wonder of His appearance among us. He would want to know if we welcome him into the humble place in our own heart or if "things" are the centerpiece of our celebration.

Frankly, I don't think He would be impressed by that big mega-church we attend where some preacher is building a monument to his ego. He would want to know if we hold regular services in our own heart or if some false prophet has convinced us He can only be found in his church or contacted through a "decision for Christ" card.

He wouldn't care a hoot how much we raised for that new building on our sprawling church but He would want to know how much we have raised for the homeless. He wouldn't care as much about how many times a week we go to church as much as how many times a week we visit a jail or nursing home or soup kitchen. I think He would be shocked to know there was a need for soup kitchens in a land that claims to be Christian. He would wonder why anyone is without a home. He would be grieved that one person is hungry.

He said his teachings were like leaven that spreads throughout the whole loaf. He would look at the loaf (America) and wonder what happened to His leaven. He would wonder why we have "God bless America" stickers instead of "God bless everyone on Earth." He would see all our big crosses signifying knowledge of His death but showing no knowledge of His life and teachings_

He would care less about how many politicians we support over posting the Ten Commandments than how many we supported who voted for justice and mercy for the handicapped, mentally ill, unemployed and the children of the poor. He would not care one whit for your sermons about free enterprise until your practice of free enterprise enabled the least among you to enterprise at all. Our talk of people needing to raise themselves by their own bootstraps would be met with a cold stare and the simple questions: What if they have no shoes? What if they have no straps? Until every deserving person gets mercy and help, he wouldn't be listening to our moralistic, immoral philosophy of greed, bias and bigotry.

He would wonder how the world made Christianity into a judgmental, powerful political army of heavy-booted holier-than-thou killers of hope and haters of the weak. He would wonder if anyone ever read the Sermon on the Mount.

What I really believe about Jesus is that the religious would want to kill him again if he came back and lived and preached the same way he lived and taught when He came before.

The good news is that anyone who wants to get out of their theology and into the simplicity of His words and His heart can still have Christmas with Him. They can still have a happy holiday and a merry, merry Christmas. They can feel the leaven He talked about and if they ever feel it, they will never have another Christmas without Him.

Miss Sallie's Boy

Sallie Crenshaw was a shiny-souled black lady who considered herself a missionary to inner city kids. Although she was an ordained United Methodist minister and spoke with a clear, rhythmic and musical tone, she always felt her main ministry was to small children.

I met her when I was heading up a youth job-training program where we took some of the toughest school dropouts and placed them in work experience places like her Good Shepherd Day Care Center.

We often referred to the "graduates" of her center as "miracle kids" because when Miss Sallie got through loving them and making them feel special, so many of them miraculously changed.

Today in my journal there was a note from her dated 1986. Her sweet little hand was trembling so much I could hardly read it. When we are awed by the great spiritual strength in people we are often shocked when their bodies start letting them down. We come to feel they are invincible. When Miss Sallie's hand started shaking all the time, I felt certain she could turn loose just a small portion of her inner power and heal herself. Despite growing feebleness, it was not possible for me to see anything but her incredible personal power until the final days of her, life.

Not long after this note, she had to go to a nursing home. I had to accept that she was getting ready to leave her body. It was not an easy thing for me to do. Before I would visit her, I would gather myself so she could have someone with calm strength to stand by her in those last hard days.

One day I commented about her skin being so dry and she asked me to massage her. I took some good oil and gave her massages during my visits. It was a special thrill to massage her sweet, angelic face. Even in her dying time she had so much radiance coming out of those sparkling eyes that I could feel it.

One day when I visited her she wanted me to wheel her out into the sunlight. I did and I cannot recall any-one loving a sunshiny day more. A soft cooling breeze and the sunlight worked a miracle on her that day. She was perkier than I had seen her in weeks.

The next time I saw her she said, "I really had some fun the last time you were here. When you left, all the patients who saw us together were asking who you were and I told them, 'He's my boy.- I will always remember that merry, mischievous chuckle. My response was, "Miss Sallie, it is such an honor for this white boy to be called one of your boys." So much of her became a part of me that I actually felt she was my second mother.

The last time I saw her stands out as both a shock and a great blessing. It was a shock to see that she could barely speak above a whisper. That melodic, musical voice was finally gone. It was a blessing because of the way she got out of her own feeling of helplessness and got into concern for me. She said, "When we do work that matters, we will be given the power to do it. Be strong and never forget the people trust you. Do not let them down. I don't believe you will."

It seemed to me that the weaker her body became, the more light emanated from her. To this day I vividly remember that strange radiance. It shines a light on my path.

She left me a big scrapbook containing some of her writings. Her words challenge me. When tempted to be less than my best, I hear her saying, "Remember, you are one of my boys." It keeps me from going astray.

The Perils of Tire Changing

Last Saturday I had a fiat tire_ I called a nearby `full service" gas station and asked them to come change it. They said they were "a little short-handed." I've never called a full service gas station in my entire life to get a tire fixed when they weren't a little short-handed.

Seeing the situation was now in the hands, of Roy Roberts' most mechanically-inclined son, I opened the trunk and found a little gizmo holding the jack and tire tool in place. I twisted it and found it was tighter than Ned's hatband.

I rubbed my frozen hands together and got a little circulation going, said a silent prayer and grabbed it again, giving it the accumulated strength from a lifetime of clean living. as well as the power of a silent prayer. The gizmo was an atheist.

Completely losing confidence in the efficacy of my prayers, I fell back upon skills that I have honed to a high level of proficiency. I started snarling and cussing.

Fate had mercy on me. I spotted a metal thing lying in the floor of the trunk, grabbed it, and gave that gizmo a Barry Bonds lick. It moved. Among the things held in place by the gizmo was a foot-long metal rod with threads on one end and a crook on the other. I saw no place to screw it or stick so I set it aside, confident I would find a place to use it.

Success in getting the jack out of the trunk, set off a trickle of endorphins in my brain, bringing the sweetest wave of tender joy to my weary heart and aching body.

I elbow-crawled under the car, hunting the right place to set the jack. They got rid of those quick, efficient, simple bumper jacks, you know. They want you to have the joy of a challenge -- the feeling an idiot has when he scales Mt. Everest, losing only a few fingers and toes to frostbite.

I finally found the right place for the jack. The turning rod would not make a complete turn without my knuckles hitting the ground so I was soon down to solid bone. I didn't notice it because my hands were frozen. The blood on the driveway tipped me off. .

When the tire finally lifted off the driveway, I was so thankful I made a promise to never cuss again or touch another drop of George Dicker.

I gave each lug a hard tug. None moved or gave the slightest hint it would ever move. I stood on the lug wrench. Then I jumped on it and the wrench flew off and struck me on the shin. I fell on the driveway, rub-bing my shin and rolling around in agony. I forgot the promise about not cussing and headed for the pantry for a straight shot of Dicker to ease the pain.

To my surprise, the leap upon the lug wrench had loosened the lug. Finding violence the key, I soon removed all the lugs. All I lost was a small piece of bone off my ankle.

I dropped the tire off at the "full service station" and went to a nearby restaurant for coffee. As I sipped, the heat in the restaurant thawed out my hands, ankles, knees, and shin. The pain began to mount. I couldn't stifle some long sighs and low moans and a lady sitting behind me said, "What is wrong with you, mister?" I smiled victoriously and answered, "I took a tire off a car, lady. By myself!" If she was impressed, I couldn't tell it.

At no point in this masterful mechanical operation did I discover what to do with the foot long rod with threads on one end and a crook on the other. If I had, I know I would have hurt myself bad trying to do it.

Little Patrick s Gift

In these times of horror stories it is easy to forget that good people are still out there every day doing good things. It is essential to fix this truth in our, minds.

Yesterday I had to speak to a group of Shriners and it reminded me of a true story from 35 years ago and my heart was warmed. I decided to share it with those Shriners.

In the sixties, I was a school social worker working with children having any kind of school adjustment problem. A teacher asked me to take a look at Patrick, a third grader who had slowly become listless.

I watched Patrick at recess. He was a typical, fun-loving boy but tired easily. The teacher had told me his father was in prison so my first thought was that he might be malnourished. When recess ended, I noticed that he had to push on his legs as he climbed the steps into the school.

His mother was pregnant and poor but said he ate well "He just seems to be losing his strength," she said.

Tests at Children's Hospital brought the heart-breaking news that he had a form of muscular dystrophy likely to cause his death in a short time. I had allowed myself to-become close to the little guy and the report just tore me down for weeks.

To make matters worse, I was unable to find any program or facility to give him the care he was sure to need.

With each passing week, my anger grew. I felt a sense of shame to live in a town where a beautiful child could not receive care during a terminal illness.

Brooding over it, I was sitting in a bar one night raving about Patrick to friends willing to listen. A stranger sitting nearby overheard me and came to my table, handing me a business card with a phone number on the back. He said, "Call that number and they will take care of the boy"

Skepticism ate at me about the man and the phone number but I did call the next day. It was the Alhambra Shrine. I described the child's predicament They took his name and address and closed the conversation exactly like the man at the bar: "Mt Roberts, we will take care of the boy."

I was stunned speechless with gratitude that someone cared. flours later, a carload of Shriners visited Patrick, taking toys and telling him about the great hospital he would soon be visiting. Two weeks later, he was taken there and for three years he returned many times for the best treatment available for his disease.

The dominant memory of those final years was the happiness he experienced in being loved by so many good men. He had dozens of fathers and they came day after day to bring him goodies and let him know he was loved. When I visited, he'd light up the room with wide-eyed wonder over it all.

As he neared the end, the doctors worked through local, health officials to make certain the pain was minimal. When he reached the end, it almost did me in. He had become like my own child despite all my efforts to remain "professional."

All griefs confer gifts if we open our hearts and eyes to see. One of my gifts was membership in the Shrine and a chance to help raise money for all the little Patricks of the world.

From the time I headed toward the East Brainerd farm of Andy Smith last night to play for the Shriners treasured memories of a little boy allowed to die happy rode with me.

Patrick, I wish you could have been there. The love in that room was as strong and real as your smile when you used to show me the gifts they brought you. They're still at it, son, pouring out hope, love and the finest medical care on every needy child -- rich or poor, black or white. I just thought you'd like to know, Little Buddy.

Taming Your Inner Shoeshine Boy

L et's put our inner shoeshine boys under the microscope and take a good look at the little aggravating rascals.

In his classic work, *The Etiology of Idiotic Inner Pests*, Dr. Zigmund Frogg wrote, "No two inner pests are alike. Each person takes the putty of poisonous personal experiences and sculpts their own inner shoeshine boy. It's not a conscious thing. It's all done by the Sleepy-eyed Prankster Within."

In explaining the problem of your inner shoeshine boy, I will keep it simple, calling upon my years of training in politics and chicken-wire joints to shake down all the professional language.

To understand the importance of taming your shoe-shine boy, it might help to look at one who got out of hand and completely took over a poor wretch.

It happened in Texas. One day a rancher was looking through binoculars at a strange-acting neighbor. He saw this neighbor putting food in a trough and leading a crawling man wearing a dog collar out on the porch to eat with the dogs.

The shocked rancher called the sheriff. Officers descended on the ranch, thinking some hapless soul was being held captive. When they finally closed in and talked to the human doggie, he was right where he wanted to be, doing exactly what he wanted to do. He had been there for years and was as happy as a human arf arf can possibly be.

It probably started with his inner shoeshine boy turning more and more back-flips to please people. If you devote your life to pleasing people, you might

meet a good old boy from Texas who has always wanted a human doggie. There's no limit to how far your shoeshine boy will go if you don't put your sharp-pointed boot deeply into the area six inches below his last lumbar vertebra.

I know you're thinking, "Oh, I'd never do some-thing like that! That is psychotic!" Most psychoses start with a neurosis getting fatter and fatter until it can huff and puff and blow your house down.

We all want to please people who change our dia-pers, powder our fannies, feed us, grade our papers and assorted other pleasantries of life. So we shine their shoes until we hear those magic words, "Good boy! Nice girl!"

Once I had a good man working for me who constantly told anyone around him, "I'm sorry" Even when he'd done something good, he'd still say "I'm sorry" because in the eyes of his inner shoeshine man, he never quite measured up no matter how well he did. One time he entered my office saying, "I'm sorry," before he said hello or gave me any idea of what he came to talk about. I broke bad and told him I'd fire him if he told me he was sorry one more time. He hung his head and said, "I'm sorry." His shoeshine man had seized that much control over him.

One of the most shocking cases - even worse than the human doggie in Texas - was a woman in New York whose father had sex with her into her thirties. A courageous, determined female prosecutor became aware of it and she dogged him and propped up the daughter's self-esteem until she was able to put the father away and see the woman start a life of her own.

This was not a retarded woman. She held a high clerical position in a demanding work situation. But her shoeshine boy had convinced her she could only have the approval of her father by complete self-subjugation.

You can confer no greater gift on a child than a deep conviction of inherent worth. Nothing else is strong enough to keep the shoeshine boy under control. Unless the child's giving and taking remain in balance, the shoeshine boy is going to set up his stand and go to work.

Finding Our Tiny Whisper

In a most unusual little magazine called "Heron Dance" I was captured by the thoughts of Jennifer Hahn. She wrote of "the tiny whisper" inside each of us. It resonated with me because I started back in the eighties trying to get in touch with my tiny whisper.

Without exception, when I speak on meditation and other ways to draw out the tiny whisper, someone will come up and say, "You don't have a regular job and that gives you the time to mess with all this inner work. If you had my job you couldn't do it."

Untrue. I started building quiet times into my day when I was running over 30 departments of county government. A health crisis drove me to try techniques to settle down the monkey mind that relentlessly drives most of us through our work days and then spills over into our off-work time, making it just as frantic and scattered as our clock-punching hours. If they ever come up with a picture dictionary, the illustration for "rat race" will be a rat with a human face chasing his own tail.

So what is this tiny whisper inside of us? Jennifer says, "The little voice is our true self"

Oh my. How can she make such a statement? Is she right? Is it possible this is not our true self zipping and zinging through busy-busy workdays? We seem to be accomplishing so much moving from one task to another at the speed of light. We can prove it. We have little "to do" lists with everything checked right off. How could we rip through such a list of responsibilities without our true self?

It's because we have created a robotic self. Robots are proficient at robotic tasks. They are not mindful.

They are not soulful. They do not feel the joy of working. But they will get you by. So if they can keep the old paychecks coming, why worry about activating the true self?

The biggest reason is there's a dimension to every job we cannot tap into without coaxing out the tiny whisper. Find times and ways to get quiet and listen to your true self impart insights about the work you are doing and the life you are living. The enhanced quality of your life will make you want to do more of it.

The true self knows you are more than an economic entity and a physiological machine. It knows you can-not find happiness working like a robot. It knows quiet and centered mindfulness brings joy to the simplest labor of head, heart or hand.

Hand work can be essential for people with head occupations. I discovered that at John C. Campbell Folk School in Brasstown, North Carolina. I have watched hyperactive, robotic people bloom like a desert rose while taking courses in woodworking, pottery or any of the skills taught there. Creative hands are a straight highway to the heart.

When we craft things, we still the mental hopscotch and the tiny whisper can be heard. Growing up I observed an aura build around my mother when she was painting. I'd see the same transformation happen when Dad cranked up his wood lathe. The very reason I talked my uncle into teaching me to play the guitar, was the special look on his face as he stroked it and sang. My tiny child whisper told me this was my soul food.

Spiritual work can also tune us into our true self. What is spiritual work but giving some time to those things we have reverence for? List the things you have reverence for and give your heart and time to them often. They are your healers.

Whatever you do, woo your tiny whisper and it will come out and talk more. If your whisper becomes your normal voice, your life will become more like a work of art. That's worth going for.

Long John Cardinal

You can get so close to an animal that it becomes a part of you. It takes on some of your traits and you take on some of its That's the way it has been with Long John Cardinal.

One morning in 1983 I saw this male cardinal trying to hang onto a feeder but constantly falling off. I got my binoculars and saw he had lost a leg. The stump looked real pink, indicating he had lost it recently.

Since he couldn't hang onto my feeders, I laid a line of sunflower seeds atop a fence on my patio and he hunkered down and ate them. Morning and night, I would put his seeds atop that fence. When I had to go out of town, my wonderful next-door neighbor, police-woman Janet Crumley, would feed him.

Cardinals may be the most skittish of all birds but Long John got so tame he would come in as I was putting out his seeds. I would talk to him and he would chirp to me in soft tones.

Knowing that cardinals only live 8 years I often said to him, "If you die, don't go off in the woods and make me worry about what happened to you. Die right here on my patio and I will give you a decent burial."

Seventeen years ago today, I went out one rainy morning and he was dead at the bottom of that fence. I buried him under the pine tree where he sat every morning waiting for me to lay out his seeds.

I don't mind telling you I cried. For five years he had been my daily companion. I had seen him raise many broods and feed them right there on my patio. It definitely increased my belief in cross-species communication when he died right where I asked him to die. If you've ever had a pet that became a constant companion for many years you will not have any difficulty accepting my belief that we can actually communicate with other species.

Long John imparted some of his very being to me. The day he died, I wrote in my journal, "Long John was drawn to me by more than his need for food. He wanted someone who could see through his one-leggedness to his spirit." That spirit became a part of my spirit. Often when I felt a lack of courage to deal with something, I would think of him and be energized. His outrage became my courage.

He wasn't my only experience in cross-species communication. One morning my wife brought me some ice water and apple cider while I was working in the garden. She said, "There's a beautiful butterfly on your sun hat." I told her that butterfly had been right with me all morning. It would get still and when I started telling it how beautiful it was it would turn around like a beauty queen as I talked and praised it. Later in the day I asked, "Do you want some cider?" and poured a few drops on my arm. It came and drank the cider. When I backed down the long driveway at the end of the day, it flew in place right in front of my windshield until I reached the road. I am telling you, I have always had this thing with butterflies.

Long John still costs me a lot of money. I have bird feeders designed to keep starlings out. One day I realized cardinals couldn't access a single feeder. So I bought a big one just for cardinals. I got to thinking that I might be depriving one of Long John's children or grandchildren with my feeding program. The black-birds get most of the seed I put in that big feeder but Long John's kids get some, too.

Isn't it beautiful for God to use a little crippled cardinal to civilize and humanize an old hairy-legged guitar picker from downtown Watering Trough?

Praying or Probleming

It might be a good idea to ask ourselves when we pray, "Am I praying or probleming?"

Probleming is pitying our aches and pains, hard times and bad luck, troubles and trials on a rotisserie and slowly turning it to make sure God is sufficiently impressed that we are a pitiful case. All the time we are reciting these things, we are actually branding problems into the very cells of our brains and fixing them in our consciousness..

Always remember the "Law of Job." He said, "That which I feared has come upon me." Tie this into "As a man thinketh so is he," and you have the "Law of Job." You can marinate in your fear so long it brings to life the very things you fear.

Sometimes we go into ridiculous detail telling God about something that is bothering us, or something we need. At such times, we are forgetting that God is omniscient, or all knowing. If our gall bladder is bothering us, do we really need to tell God where the pain starts and where it shoots and how often the pain occurs? Paul said "we live and move and have our being in Him." If God is the very Life Force in which we exist, there is a good chance He knows just about anything we can tell Him about our aches and pains.

One of the shortest prayers in the Bible came from

the lips of a man who had more problems that we will ever experience. He was a thief. He was dying. He was nailed to a crossbeam of wood with big nails in both wrists and both feet. He simply prayed, "Lord, remember me," and Jesus said, "This day you will be with me in paradise." Jesus didn't say, "Tell me more about your problems, pal." He knew exactly how the man felt and He knows exactly how we feel. As one writer said, "He is touched with the feeling of our infirmities" because He "was tempted in all points like as we are."

I love the word "cast" in "cast your burden upon the Lord." It doesn't take long to cast something. It doesn't say "describe your burden in infinite detail to the Lord because He must be completely convinced before He will help you." It's not like checking into the emergency room of a hospital where they want reams of information while you sit there and die. All it takes to check into God's ER is, "Lord, remember me."

One of the best changes I have made in my mornings is insisting on some total quiet. Someone has said, "Prayer is talking to God and, meditation is listening to God." I have witnessed this truth in my own life. Before I touch the morning paper, the TV, radio or CD player, I get still and quiet for a while. It puts me in touch with the God of my being and I think that is the only place we ever meet God.

Getting quiet and still often imparts thoughts of wisdom and guidance but when it does not result in clear-cut guidance, it still provides a priceless time for fellowship with God and fresh oil for our lamps.

Once a goofy tape I made for a few crazy friends, I said of problems, "When you have a problem, it is only in one gourd - yours - but when you tell me about it, you place it in two gourds and double its power." While admitting we often have to talk to someone or explode, I still insist there is crazy wisdom in that statement. You can walk through a big building and tell a problem to everyone you meet and you psychologically bring the whole building to its knees.

Tell the God of your inner being - the good news every morning. Then say, "Here are some things we need to work on. So, Lord, remember me."

Set Aside Days to Listen

A reader reminded me of the personal pleasure in learning to listen. She wrote, "Blessed rain falls slowly. I love the pitter-patter as it dances on the roof. Wind chimes softly tinkling. Sweet morning. I sit here in this quiet room listening to the rain and the old clock ticking."

See how engrossed she is in listening? She hears it all - the rain, the wind chimes and the clock. She

doesn't mention listening to the inner unfolding of her own thoughts but once you learn to listen, that is life's extra gift to you.

Learning to really listen was a mid-life thing for me. I set aside a morning quiet time to do breathing exercises to lower my blood pressure. Over time I varied the breathing exercises with other meditative activities like bird watching, journaling and a half dozen other techniques but the one constant was a time of stillness and quietness.

Surprisingly, it helped my emotions more than my blood pressure. I went into my day centered, calm and joyous. I was more effective in handling the hectic schedule I had at that busy time of my life. I started off with 15 minutes of quiet and in a short time I was setting aside a full hour. It became indispensable to me because of the deep peace and quiet focus it imparted.

I had no idea how scattered I had been until that

time. It never occurred to me that I needed to slow down and quietly observe my world and my own thoughts. I had always hit the floor running. As the morning stillness did it's miraculous work on me, I could look back and see that when I hit the floor running, I was often running on empty.

A wonderful result of this change in lifestyle was the immense increase in creative ideas. I realized I was contacting a deeper dimension of myself - the layer of consciousness where creative solutions are born.

Yes, it started with 15 minutes, and then became an hour and now I have listening days! The best way to sharpen your listening skills is to set aside a listening day. I mean, schedule it. Note it on your daily agenda.

It doesn't have to be a day you are off from work. Maybe the first couple of listening days might work better if you are off from work but when you get the hang of it you will find it works just as well on a workday.

On your listening days, don't be surprised if people notice a difference in the quality of your energy_ You will feel it, too, as surely as a solar cell feels the power of the sun.

As you develop the habit of really listening to people they will seek your companionship more often. One of the rarest things on this planet is a person who really listens to people. Try to tell a short story about some experience and you will be lucky if you get through it. As soon as you start, you will remind someone of their own story and they will interrupt you until you forget your own story!

When we listen, we are often only half-listening. The other half of our brain is trying to think of what we can say when the talker gets through.

With listening days, you can break this pattern. Really listen to everyone you meet all day. You will certainly have some times of boredom because not everyone is a ball of fire. But do it for yourself as well as those you meet all day. You are giving yourself the priceless gift of listening.

In time, you may hear some amazing things like Rodney Crowell mentions in his "Song of Life." He wrote, "Somehow I've learned how to listen, to the sound of the sun going down." He had graduated from listening with his ears to listening with his soul.

Honor your Feelings

There is nothing harder in a personal spiritual practice than the gnawing feeling that you are making little if any progress. You often feel you are just thrashing around in the water and not swimming. You seem to be just where you were long ago. Discouragement gets so thick you can cut it with a knife.

Is the problem that we expect too much of ourselves? Or is it that we expect too much of life? Is it possible to expect too much of God?

To be honest, I do not know. I wish I had some hocus-pocus to lay on you. I wish I could just pop you and me on the forehead and we would be healed of these feelings of deep discouragement.

For years I have read writings of great mystics on "the dark night of the soul." I don't know exactly what it is. For me it has often taken the foam of that gnawing feeling that I am not making much progress, that I am just thrashing around in the water.

Mother Teresa said something about not trying to do great things but to do little things with great devotion. That's what I try to do. When the wet blanket drops on me, I try to just do one small thing with mindfulness. I mean, something as tiny as giving a pint of blood, or making a small anonymous contribution to some good cause. One tiny thing a day until the feeling passes.

Maybe the most spiritual thing we will ever do is revel in our smallness. To acknowledge that we are not big shots or hotshots. I am not saying we should debase ourselves but is there any spirituality in straining? Can we not learn to flow with the slow times, to accept where we are? Can we become more until we accept where we are and how we feel?

Jesus said those who are faithful over a little would be given more. Maybe that is the key.

I keep thinking of the Englishman who asked that these words be placed on his tombstone: "Here lies John Smyth who cobbled shoes in this town 40 years to the glory, of God."

Nothing is Ever Lost

My friend Sparky had a terrific dream in which everything he had ever owned was returned to him. We talked about what the dream meant and I told him I thought the clear message was that nothing is ever lost.

There Sparky was in his dream walking around looking at every car he had ever owned, walking down the street and going into every house where he had lived over his years, going into rooms with every toy he had ever owned, sitting once again on the seat of every shiny bicycle he had been given as a child.

It is possible to enjoy so deeply and spiritually the people and things that come into our lives that no life development can take them from us, not even death. It is not the people who love shallowly who get over losing things more quickly. It's the people who drink in life so deeply that it all becomes a part of their very being.

You have heard people say things like, "I will never love that much again. It hurts too bad to lose someone who becomes dear and precious to us."

Baloney. That's all I've got to say to such love rationers. You are short-changing and cheating people who want to love you. They will sense you are holding back. They will see you are emotionally crippled.

Worse yet, you are robbing yourself of a chance to

fully experience life. Who enjoys a glass of wine the most --
a man who chugs it down thoughtlessly or a man who
slowly sips and deeply savors each drop? Every drop of life
that comes your way is meant to be savored by your body,
mind and soul.

Don't let your possessions possess you but pos-sess
their essence so completely that they can never be taken
from you. This may be a hard saying but it is a truth that
can be understood through a very simple story.

I wrote songs in Nashville for many years and got
caught up in the politics of the music business until it
embittered me. I was not writing songs that came from my
inner being. I was writing what the "pros" in the business
told me had the best chance to be recorded. Few of those
songs mean much to me. I seldom sing them. 'I was not
writing them for me so they never became a part of me.
Then in 1994 I decided to write what I wanted to write,
produce my own sessions exactly like I thought the songs
should sound, and those songs are all like my children. I
love them and sing them_ It feels like each new song
becomes a part of my colorful quilt of life.

I was talking to songwriter Malcolm Holcombe one
night and telling him some of my songs that have been
recorded by the stars. I said, "If I had stayed in Nashville
and kept writing, I think I would have had a lot of hits, but
I got into politics and lost my music contacts." Malcolm
said, "Man, nothing is ever lost."

All of life is just exploring different realities. If you
leave songwriting for politics, your experience in poli-tics
will just add different angles, perspectives, colors and
insights to your songwriting when you return to it. When
I look at the songs I have written since 1994, I can see this
so clearly.

Love the people around you with all your heart and your heart will keep them alive for you even if they die. If you don't love them with all your heart, your heart will not be able to make them real to you.

Love as much of your Work as you possibly can, even if it's not your first choice, and it will enrich you financially and spiritually. Make your motto, "I shall possess the essence of my life experiences and their beauty will be mine forever."

A Preacher I Wish I Had Taped

Some readers have written that my preacher stories were hard to believe. Except for names where I thought family members might be embarrassed, every one of them has been true. But if you had trouble believing the previous ones, today's will really be hard for you to believe.

Unknown to me, the preacher who tiptoed for Jesus in Nashville and dragged chains down the aisle, moved to Chattanooga for his final years. One day I saw him in the hall at the courthouse and he said, "I remember you coming to my revivals around Nashville." He seemed impressed that I had been elected county executive.

One day near Christmas I was picking up a huge cake I wanted to take to the Orange Grove Singers who had recorded one of my Christmas songs and the lady at the cake place told me it would be 25 minutes before it would be ready. I said, "Well, I'll just walk the mall for 25 minutes."

Halfway through my first round, I ran into the preacher again. He yelled, "Stop! Oh, thank God (he pronounced it 'Guide') I have run into you this morning. Guide revealed to me that you were going to be the man to do a movie on my life and to videotape my final sermon for planet Earth."

I froze and thought, "What I would give to have a

tape recorder in my shirt pocket because this is going to be something unbelievable."

He continued, "I'm going to take you back to where I grew up and to the very place where Guide called me to preach. I was just seven years old and had never even heard of Guide."

"See this scar right here?" he said, pointing to a deep indentation in his forehead, "That's where a mule kicked me right after Guide called me. See this scar right here?" he asked, pointing to a scar under his chin, "That's where a limb stuck deep into my throat, both things happening within a week of Guide calling me to preach, brother!"

I said, "Where was Guide while this was going on?" and he said, "Testing me, brother!"

Honestly, I thought it a little strange that God would call a seven year old boy to preach and then test him

Bertie Never Lost Her Place in a Song

In today's true story, the names have been changed to protect the innocent, the guilty and the unconscious.

For a while I played music in a nice little place where violence was discouraged. It was such a pleasant place I often went there on days when I was not performing. It attracted a lot of musicians who liked to sit around and jam.

One of my favorite jam buddies was Bertie Hancock. She was a big-boned blonde who played guitar pretty well and sang a lot of the old country songs of Molly O'Day and Kitty Wells. She loved the old gospel song, "Wait A Little Longer Please Jesus."

Bertie's main squeeze was a guy everyone called "Dapper Dan." He was a little smaller than her and had a thin-line mustache. Bertie was clearly jealous of him and I never saw him solicit the attention of other women because he didn't want to rile Bertie.

One day she and I were sitting in a booth jamming and she got around to Wait a Little Longer Please Jesus. Suddenly, right in the middle of the song she calmly said, "Excuse me, Dalton," and propped her guitar up in the booth. She walked toward the stool where an intoxicated female customer was draped over Dapper Dan. Everything got quiet except the jukebox as Bertie said to the woman, "Excuse me, Hon." She took her firmly by both shoulders, turned her just right, and came up with the most lethal uppercut I have ever seen. She dropped that woman in her tracks. I mean one lick and she was out.

This intruder into Dapper Dan's space was completely unconscious. I know because her toes were wiggling and I had seen the toes of prizefighter's twitch on TV when they went down for the count. Someone brought a cold towel and it was a while before the old gal fully regained consciousness.

Bertie calmly rejoined me in the booth, picked up her guitar and returned to the exact location in the lyric of Wait A Little Longer Please Jesus as when she left to take care of business. It struck me as funny that someone could pause in a gospel song, knock someone out and go right back to where they left the lyric. I laid down my guitar and doubled up in laughter.

Bertie said, "What's so funny?" and I answered, "You came back to the place in the song where you left off, Bertie." She said, "Well, what was I supposed to do, big boy?" I didn't say anything smart to her. I didn't want to see that uppercut coming my way.

Over the years I became fonder of Bertie out of respect for her complete authenticity. She was a good person, a pretty good singer and picker and, like Tammy Wynette, she stood by her man.

Twenty years later I was visiting Senator's to hear some friends when they had a request for a Hank Williams song. They knew how much I loved Hank and called me up to do "Cold Cold Heart." As I walked back to my seat a young man came up and embraced me, sobbing so hard his whole body was shaking.

"My Mama always said you could sing Hank Williams and she was right," he said between sobs. I asked,

"Who is your Mama, son," and he replied, "Bertie Hancock. She died two years ago."

I was surprised to feel warm tears running down my cheeks. I suddenly realized how much affection I had for Bertie. Maybe it was just the sharing of music but I really think there was more to it. She was one of the most genuine, honest human beings I have known.

Bertie would love a thought I had when Mike Tyson was accused of rape. I thought how funny it would have been if Tyson had tried to force himself on Bertie. I can see his toes twitching now.

The Power of Honest Intention

Carl Jung wrote, "Your vision will become clear only when you look into your heart. Who looks outside, dreams. Who looks inside, awakens."

I love Rev. Angelica Jayne's Friday messages. In a recent one she talked about intention and how intention triggers your creative subconscious mind to bring forth solutions.

She talked about a client who wanted her life work to become clearer to her so she declared; "It is my intention to do the work I came here to do." Just declaring her intention triggered her creative mind to open doors and make her path clear.

I know this works. I once sat in a one-room apartment, freshly-fired and even more freshly divorced. I was an agnostic at that time but I did declare my intention with a simple prayer, "God, if you are real, open a door for me. My way of seeing if you exist will be open doors. When a door is slammed on me, I will not try to kick it open. I will simply look for open doors and if you help me find a life, I will serve you and my fellow man with integrity."

Within weeks, a door opened for me to run for the highest office in the county. Though I was broke, I was elected.

I discovered the power of making an honest statement to God. I wasn't demanding. Just declaring the intention of my heart and mind. God always has and always will honor our honest intentions. And one method He uses to respond is through our creative mind.

The doors that opened for me to make that race were clearly surprises. Some would call them miracles. Contrary to our human addiction to flashiness, some miracles are just quiet out workings. The reason I saw them as miracles was that there was no logical, rational reason to expect them to happen. When you declare an honest intention to do good and to live your life for God, you will definitely see some miraculous but quiet out workings.

It's not so much that God takes time off from a million planetary concerns, as it is our use of divine laws. The Universe is lawful. It operates according to certain natural and spiritual laws. The spiritual law of declaring your intention and activating your creative mind is as certain as the law of gravity.

The second miraculous outworking in my situation was the awakening that Jung mentioned. I was only watching for open doors but I learned that keeping inwardly awake to the whisperings of creative mind was the way to find constant awareness. It tunes you in to the prompts of Spirit.

Jung says those who look outside, dream. They usually dream of things they want. There are times we need things but even at those times, the path to attainment is to awaken inside. Stay honestly open, keeping your motivations under continual review.

When I was running, .I kept my inner motivation pure. I really had one dominant desire and that was to serve God and people. To keep selfishness and other base motivations from entering our spiritual lifeblood, we must remain in tune with our highest inner nature.

The sweetest result of declaring an honest intention and listening to our inner guidance is a growing awareness of the constant presence and fellowship of the Spirit of God. It made me an incurable mystic. A mystic bases his spiritual value system on his own personal experience. I knew for the first time in my life that the presence of the Lord is as real as any experience we can have in this life. It was not something I expected. It was a life-changing surprise.

I do not talk about my personal experience to brag on myself. You cannot brag on yourself when you know your success is due to stumbling into a spiritual law and discovering what it can do.

With gratitude, I witness to you that it is true.

My Possum Peace Plan

It had to happen. In this age of violence with guns popping like omnipresent popcorn and nuclear bombs pointing toward every place on the planet worth wiping out, someone just had to come up with the perfect way to end human killing and bring peace to human-kind. I just never thought it would be me.

It was given to me -- a "eureka" that came one day as I contemplated the hidden beauty of the possum The plan requires only two commitments from world leaders. It will not only stop wars and homicides in a short while, it will stimulate the planetary economy and, improve muscle tone among the people.

Anthropologists say the possum was one of the few animals to survive the awful catastrophe that destroyed all the dinosaurs except Strom Thurmond. They figure that a huge terrestrial body collided with Earth, making a cloud of dust that closed off the sun for weeks, sloshed the oceans over the land and wiped out all the green stuff.

In case you question the scientists or just can't picture this happening, imagine an ant sitting on a tennis ball traveling 570,000 miles an hour crashing into a basketball going even faster. The dinosaur's that weren't slammed to death against trees and rocks died of starvation or were hurled out beyond Earth's gravitational field and are still zooming through space mumbling, "Somebody put something in my drink!"

Think about it -- the possum survived that mind-boggling event! He just kept turning over garbage cans, eating coffee grounds and potato peels, and stayed fat.

Point one of the Possum Peace Plan is to get a UN commitment that every nation lay down arms of all kinds and use nothing but wet possums to attack other persons or nations or to defend themselves or their territories. The NRA will become the NPA, lobbying all over the world for people's right to carry as many possums as they can feed. Possum breeders will come up with longer snouts and more teeth. Pick-up trucks will no longer have gun racks. Possum cages will be standard equipment.

People are inherently lazy. They are killing each other off simply because it is so easy. Force them to go get a possum and dip it in a tank of water before they beat someone to death and the prospects for peace brighten dramatically. Yes, there will still be some killings. Even a few wars. The Mid East will be a major possum market for a while. But sitting here thinking back over my troubled life, I can think of precious few people I might possum to death.

Point two is that every person who whacks a wet possum to death in battle or any homicide, has to cook and eat it. If you've ever eaten one, you know it will not take long for this policy to eliminate violence.

When I was a lad, I was visiting the home of a neighborhood widower whose two sons were beer-sucking buddies. A possum was cooking on the kitchen woodstove and there was at least a solid inch of grease gurgling atop the flesh and sweet potatoes. As lack of luck would have it, it was one of the few times he ever invited me to join them for dinner.

A few years ago I underwent psychiatric counseling for an old broken heart. I asked the kind doctor if he could do anything to help me get over the memory of eating that possum in my tender teens and he said, "Freud postulated that the memory of the taste of pos-sum was more intractable than being thrice-dipped in a boiling cauldron of used motor oil." I got over the woman but that possum is still hanging on the nipple of my brain stem.

When peace finally comes, for the first time since Earth came spinning out of the Big Bang, it will be high class to be a possum.

The Gifts of a Great Father

Today I had two realizations. One is that next Sunday is Father's Day. The other is that my father passed away nine years ago today.

Reflecting on his death and the 57 years I knew him as my father, my heart bows in respect for the gifts he gave. If every child born this day had a father like mine, this world would be a heaven on Earth.

The quality of mothering on this planet is much superior to the quality of fathering. Biology may be part of the reason. For nine months, mothers are tethered to their babies as they grow inside their bodies. If the mother is anywhere near normal in intelligence, character and mental health, there is a bonding process here beyond the ability of any words to describe.

My father bonded with his children. I' know it from one of my favorite pictures of him, taken just hours after my birth at my Aunt Carrie's home in Danville, Alabama. He carried me to a grocery store up the road to weigh me and someone there took our picture. The smile in the photograph made me know I was starting off affirmed and protected in this strange new world where I had just landed.

A mental picture I treasure equally came from something Mother told me in my late thirties. Dad told her not to tell us but she thought we ought to know and correctly decided it would enhance our appreciation for him.

During the worst days of the Great Depression he jumped freights all over the South searching for a job to feed his wife and two little girls. In Florida he was arrested and jailed. When I see him in my mind's eye hanging onto the side of a fast moving train in the dark night with cold wind whistling through old work clothes washed weary in roadside creeks, plodding with steel will his pilgrim way from town to town in thirsty search for any kind of work, my cup runs over with admiration and love.

When I remember that he became a minister in 1923 at the age of sixteen and never took a drink of liquor or smoked a cigarette in his life, and then imagine him sitting behind bars because he loved his family so much, tears always well up in my eyes. One day when I was County Executive 'I got to thinking about it in the middle of my workday. I just canceled my appointment for the rest of the day and drove over to the old home place to give my little Daddy a big hug.

In the building where this newspaper is now published, my father worked for 27 years with Davenport Hosiery Mill. He landed a job as a knitter just weeks before I was born. The knitting machines were made in Germany and when Kurt Esch came over to work on them, no one could communicate with him in German. Dad taught himself to speak German in a short time and he would talk for hours with Esch to improve his skills.

He pastored several small churches and was a grand orator, stringing out beautiful words like God painting a hillside with wildflowers. But being a minister was just part of his calling. His other calling was to demonstrate the equal sacredness of working with his hands. He was an artist with a wood lathe and equally proficient at carpentry, plumbing or auto mechanics. If he'd pastored the biggest church in the country, he would have never considered that more holy than crawling under a Volkswagen.

I visited him one day at lunch when he was a machinist at Standifer Nissan. . He was chewing on a sandwich and his dog-eared German Bible with equal delight.

I wish I could visit him Sunday but it's not necessary. He's with me all the time and has turned every day of my life into Father's Day.

It's Okay for Hillbillies to Meditate

An urban planner from New York once said to me, "I hear you meditate. I would have never thought a guitar-picking politician from Tennessee would be a meditator."

I didn't know whether to feel offended or complimented. But she had called me "a renaissance redneck," so I didn't want to flare up on someone who might be trying to bestow a compliment.

A mental picture of a hillbilly in overalls sitting by is moonshine still in the lotus position flashed into my mind and a good chuckle saved the day. I simply answered, "Yes, Ma'am, I guess there's no law that says hillbillies and rednecks can't meditate, too."

Strange as it may appear to anyone whose mental boat has got stuck on an old iceberg stereotype, this old hillbilly has been meditating for over a decade. It started when I read a news story showing that meditators showed considerable drops in blood pressure to non-mediators.

In my library I found a book on breath meditation. t11-1-.rj. 60' ath exere,   -I n d i t w a s probably ,fcic ticst   breat   -nee high school basketball. The oxygen was delicious. Best of all, the old blood pressure dropped a little.

Books by Catholic and Buddhist monks became my

best source of information. Some claimed the attainment of transcendent states of consciousness. I found one good book by a medical doctor who teaches a "relaxation response."

Some were high on mantras - special words or phrases that induce a relaxed state of mind. Transcendental Meditation teaches students to adopt their own personal mantra. I respect their expertise but I decided to develop my own way of meditating. Hillbillies are independent like that.

Words are wonder workers. If you had good parents, say the word "Mama" or "Daddy," and notice the warm blanket it ells over your body and mind. Any word will do so long as it is a word that means something special to you.

In a marvelous little book titled Indian Love Letters, I discovered the Hopi word "lolomi." It is my all-time favorite word. It means "everything warm and wonderful beyond the ability of words to express." As you piddle -- and by all means do piddle -- through the tapes and films of your own life experiences, you will find words that work as well for you. Roll them around on the tip of your soul tongue until you find those that taste just right for you.

Many accomplished meditators use mandalas - pictures, drawings, objects or icons that smooth you out, ease your mind, lift your spirit and bring a big soul-satisfying smile. My favorite mandala is a sculpture of my one-legged, five-year bird companion, Long John Cardinal, that my daughter sculpted for me. Anything will do so long as it rings your own joy bells.

Walking meditations work real well for me. If I need peace and calm, I walk very slowly, immersing myself in the beauty of trees, flowers, pine needles, butterflies, grasshoppers and anything I see along the way. If I need invigoration and expansion, I walk briskly feeling a oneness with the birds and breezes of the day.

One that grafts you into the moment in an incredible way is slow-motion mediation.. Just intentionally slow down to a surreal level while doing household chores or gardening and pay complete attention to every de-tail of what you are doing. The more you do this one, the more you will find yourself soaking up the right-nows of your life.

Another trick is identifying with something in your field of vision. Get out of you for a while. Become the Goldfinch eating sunflower seed. Taste it and when it leaves, feel the wind under your wings. Keep doing it until you no longer feel self-conscious about it.

Yes, it can lower your blood pressure and, yes you can do it. If a hillbilly can do it, anyone can.

Decide What is "Success" for You

Each of us has a little ruler in our mind that measures our success. It's important to know whether it's someone else's ruler or our own.

If your only measurement is money, my heart hurts for you. In "Upside Down," Eduardo Galeano wrote, "Children today are denied to be children. The world treats rich kids as if they were money, teaching them to act the way money acts. The world treats poor kids as if they were garbage, to turn them into garbage. And those in the middle, neither rich nor poor, are chained to televisions and trained to live the life of prisoners."

All these kids are denied the highest and best. Personal fulfillment and service to humanity are the only two paths to the good life.

The part of the quote we are most likely to miss is the sentence about rich kids. They are treated as if they are money and expected to act as money acts. While some people do have the gift and ministry of making money, those who make money a god to their kids sin against their souls.

Neither should we transmit a notion of poverty as a worthy goal, or conformity to values touted by television and society's other mighty message-senders.

To me, one of the meanings of being "born again" is to make an instantaneous and total change of values and then stay with it. All the years I served in political office, I was reluctant to talk about spiritual things.

It turns people off for politicians to talk religion. But the time has come for me to give credit where credit is due and the credit for any success I experienced in the worthwhile work of politics goes to the Lord.

Sitting in a one room apartment after being fired and unable to find a job, I turned my life over to God. My theology might not fall into the norm for this area, or any other area, but our spiritual experiences are always our own. You may accept my word or reject it, but I must tell you there is no question at all in my mind that God was with me during that time of my life and gave me the strength, vision and joy to succeed.

The advantage of that decision was that I no longer had to measure my success. It was no longer any of my business. I had turned that over to God. There were times when ego made me think of grabbing it back but it's just too good a deal as it is. No worry about how well I am doing, how much money I am making, or how much recognition I am getting. All I have to do is live out my talents (another word for "callings"), stay clear in my heart and soul and accept open doors as signs of what I should do next.

Until my last breath, I will thank God for the honor of working for the people but I began to feel an irresistible tug in another direction. Many people thought I shouldn't quit. The chairman of the opposition party had already told me they were not going to run anyone against me. I had a great staff and we were moving forward with all kinds of exciting projects. But I knew the time had come to write and perform. Those, too, were callings from my earliest years.

I've not made a lot of money. One of my heroes, songwriter/singer Gail Davies, expresses my sentiments perfectly: "A friend of mine once told me never to confuse reward with compensation, because the reward is knowing you did your job the best you could do it. The compensation is what other people give you. Sometimes I have to remind myself that the Mona Lisa was a masterpiece because it was painted, not because it was sold."

Check the ruler in your mind. Better still, just take it out.

Baby Girl and the Biker

I am not a cardiologist, but I choose a friend by the quality of their heart. I think Jerry Hall will always be my friend. I didn't have to check out his heart. Baby Girl did it for me.

Baby Girl is a five year old Boston Terrier. Her original owners went out of town for several days and left her chained up with no food or water. Neighbors called the Humane Society but no one came to help her. She finally climbed a fence trying to get to dog food in the yard next door and was left dangling there by her dog collar so long it that all the skin on her neck was worn off.

That neighbor took her to a veterinarian who said she might not live. She was full of worms and dangerously malnourished. One person who saw her at this time called her "a walking skeleton."

Jerry owns That Bike Shop on Highway 58 and one of his friends was asked by Baby Girl's rescuer to help find her a home. Jerry had never owned a dog but the story of Baby Girl's short life got to him He asked his friend to bring the dog to her nearby dog grooming business so he could see if they liked each other.

The first day Jerry spent a lot of time with Baby Girl. She slowly warmed up to him but he was still undecided about buying her because he got no clear sign from her. The second day he rode his Honda Gold Wing motorcycle to work and went back to check

out Baby Girl. When he got ready to leave, Baby Girl went wild and pulled on her leash so hard they let her loose and she ran straight for the motorcycle, jumping up on the seat.

Jerry says it was like she staked her claim on that motorcycle seat. He decided to take her for a test ride. He says, "As I rode her around I could tell she loved the motorcycle. We swapped a few kisses and I knew I had me a riding partner. I love to take trips -- just ride and see the country and had always wanted someone to go with me. Baby Girl became my trip buddy that first day and has been with me all over the country ever since."

To make it safe and comfortable for her, he secured a milk tray to his bike and lined it with fake fur. Instead of a collar which might evoke some painful old memories for her, he outfitted her with a chest harness. It allows her to move around in her riding area.

Jerry takes Baby Girl to all kinds of biker events and says, "People may not know me but they know her. As soon as I pull in I can hear them saying, 'Hey! Here comes Baby Girl!'"

The first time I saw Jerry and Baby Girl I was having breakfast at the Waffle House on Highway 58. He pulled up and secured his bike right outside the window. Naturally I thought it unusual to see a dog bed on the back of a motorcycle but what I saw next was more unusual. This big biker removed his helmet, then walked back and kissed his dog and nuzzled her like he was telling her goodbye. She kissed him back, then snuggled down in her bed while he came in and ate.

Jerry didn't sit facing Baby Girl and I never saw him

check on her. He knows she will stay in her place on the bike. And she did. Several diners would stop as they came or went and pet her a little. She clearly enjoyed the attention.

I thank the neighbors who rescued Baby Girl as she hung suspended on that fence. They saved her life, added lots of love to many lives (like mine), and gave Jerry Hall a bike buddy for life.

Loving What Is

Spinoza said, "Become a lover of what is" and if we don't, what is will keep grinding us to a little pile of powder as long as we live.

This thought hit me powerfully when I was reading a great book by Byron Katie titled, *Loving What Is* (Harmony Books, 2002), at the same time I received a note from a dear friend. You know, one of those coincidences you feel is a higher power talking to you. As I wrote in my book *Kickstarts*, "Coincidences are God's way of saying 'howdy.'"

Katie's book hit me like a Louisville Slugger. I read it three times before I was able to pass it on to my sister who wanted to read it. If you've had the tendency to worry yourself half-crazy over people you love sabotaging themselves, you might profit from reading it and answering the four questions she applies to every troubling thought: Is it true? Can you absolutely know it is true? How do you react when you think that thought? And how would you feel without that thought? Then she teaches you to do a "turnaround" of the thought.

It may sound like a yawningly simple formula for personal peace. It is simple but you will do no yawning when you start to apply it to the thorns in your mind. Like me, you may wind up doing more soul-searching than you expected.

At the same time I was reading and re-reading Katie's

book, a long-time friend wrote me about a mutual acquaintance. She was worried because this person has taken so many "hard falls." When we see this Humpty Dumpty cycle in someone's life, we always wonder how many times they can crash without giving up.

As the old rhyme says, there does come a time when Humpty can't put himself together again.

One of life's deepest heart-stabs is seeing this vicious cycle in people we love. I don't mind admitting I have no magic wand answers. All I know to do is to keep caring for them without getting in their blenders.

We become paralyzed by the question, "Why do they keep doing this to themselves?" We may have all kinds of theories and may even be highly trained in behavioral sciences, but the fundamental fact is, they don't know and we don't know. The true reasons can be buried in their psyches, their pasts or even in their metabolisms.

Katie says, "You are the teacher you have been waiting for." Meaning that no change in Humpty Dumptyism can possibly be made until the person becomes self-observational and starts digging within for answers. That ferreting-out process may require the aid of a professional but it must become a regular life-groove to succeed.

Often our involvement with those we view as self-saboteurs comes from us trying to impose our life purpose on them. Katie speaks to that: "Maybe their life shouldn't have a purpose other than to do what is in front of them." People do not need our grandiose schemes for their lives.

As weird as the thought might be to those who have a rigid view of normalcy, we might remind ourselves now and then that some of the greatest contributors to humankind have been very un-normal people. We might ask ourselves if taking our path would despoil their uniqueness. Maybe they are needed as they are to give the status quo a karate chop or to wrestle some big-horned sacred cows to the ground.

Eric Hoffer said, "You accept certain unlovely things about yourself and manage to live with them. The atonement for such an acceptance is that you make allowances for others."

Loving and respecting someone as they are is surely the first step in helping them change, in case they really need to change, which is really their business.

If your omniscience needs a good healthy jolt, and you want some practical tools to help you accept what is, read Katie's book.

Life is a Thump-Ripe Melon

A line jumped out at me from one of Greg Brown's folk songs! -Life is like a thump-ripe melon. So sweet and such a mess."

My mother told about a man who could sec nothing but the sweetness. He never said a critical word about anyone. His friends got disgusted with his knee-jerk positive attitude and decided to give him the ultimate test by asking him if he saw anything good about the Devil. He rubbed his chin and thought a few seconds and said, "Well, I will say one thing for him. He stays busy."

One problem common to those who see nothing but the sweetness is that they don't clean up the messes. They repress awareness of them. If you're lost in bliss you ignore anything that threatens your swim in the waters of Lake Ecstasy. Neither will you join forces with groups committed to cleaning up society's mess-es. Do not expect "bliss-ters" to volunteer at the soup kitchen or run in a charity marathon.

Bliss babies are really pretty useless. Evasion of life unpleasantries does not make them go away. It merely cripples the ability to cope. That which we do not face we do not deal with effectively.

Think of the incredible level of repression bliss babies experience every day. One thing we know for sure about repression is that repressed thoughts express in unhealthy ways. It's like pushing ping pong balls to the bottom of a barrel of water. They will come up and they will burst in your face.

On the other hand, I bet you know someone who is totally into seeing life as a mess. There's a lot more of these lemon suckers than bliss babies. Recently a family member told me about spending 35 years trying to get a dear friend to see the bright side of one situation. Her efforts were in vain. Her friend saw the worst in everything and everybody. She was a loyal and true friend but could not see anyone else as equally good and worthy.

Maybe it is the silly end of this sweetness-mess issue but I found myself not buying watermelons because I didn't like to pick out the seeds. I tried one of the seedless watermelons. They taste pretty decent but my taste buds report they are not as sweet as the seeded ones (there I go being a negative thinker!). So I went back to the seeded melons and worked on my seeding technique. I found that slicing them into skinny sections enables you to quickly pop out the seeds.

I actually had a dream that I was a watermelon de-seeder for a king. When I missed a seed and His High and Mightiness had to spit it out, he got me slapped around. That's where I got the idea for the skinny slices. I actually thought of it in that dream If you are a college student and trying to make a decision on a career, I do not recommend watermelon de-seeding. You can wind up like John the Baptist with your cantaloupe head on a platter.

Life really is a thump-ripe melon just like Greg Brown sang. It is so sweet and such a mess. We can only avoid the mess by avoiding the experience of the sweetness. That is too big a price to pay.

One idea like thin-slicing a melon to reveal the seeds

and make them easier to remove can make a big difference in accentuating the sweetness and minimizing the mess. Ever notice the happiest people are those who go around collecting good ideas?

I have discovered that the key to the good life is en-joying the mess as well as the sweetness. I recall a picture of a small child eating a big slice of watermelon with a large smile and juice dripping off his chin. Now what could be more beautiful? If only he knew he had just found the secret to enjoying all of life.

We Can Transcend Grief

Since I started writing this column some years ago, nothing has surprised me more than the response I got to the one on funerals being a potential source of spiritual strength. The biggest part of this eye-opener was the number of people who have remained locked in grief for years.

Shakespeare said in Much Ado About Nothing, "Everyone can master a grief but he that has it." So let me speak not from a perch of superiority but from the hard ground of grief where we all stand several times in a normal lifespan. Let me simply share the thoughts that have helped me make it through the fog to a friendly port.

The thing to do with grief is to grieve. Like Euripides, we sometimes pray, "Oh to be a stone! To feel no grief!" but that is a closure of the heart. We will not find relief until we open ourselves to the feelings welling up deep inside, wailing like a wounded animal in a cave seeking to be known and heard.

As William Cowper wisely spoke, "Grief is itself a medicine." Trouble is, there are times when we cannot take the medicine. Sometimes other emotions are blowing through us with an intensity equal to our grief.

I experienced this with the passing of my mother. Her final 16 days in the hospital were so horrendous that we were praying she would find respite. When she died, I was so relieved she was out of the wires and tubes that I could not cry.

She had always written us birthday letters and a year after her death I was dining alone and reading my mail when I came across an early birthday card. The thought came, "You will never get another birthday letter from your mother."Scalding tears started trickling down my cheeks and in few moments I could not control the flow. I left the money for my tab on the table and left. For hours I walked the floor and sobbed.

It's losing those endearing, special things that hit us hardest. One thing we can do to transcend this kind of shattering sorrow is to do those endearing, special things ourselves. I started writing letters on my birthday. Sometimes I send a check in mother's memory to those who care for the homeless, stray animals or injured birds. Mother never turned away a hobo needing a meal, or an abandoned child or animal. She would feed and nurse injured birds knowing they would probably die and break her tender heart.

You see, that just it. Some birds die no matter how much we want them to live. Unless we are willing to have a broken heart, we are not fully human. Pouches of precious spices must be punctured for their aroma to be released. Love is often released more powerfully from a broken heart than from one that is whole.

There is no more beautiful verse in the New Testament than "Jesus wept." His friend Lazarus had died and left his two sisters broken-hearted. He was a special friend of Jesus. Jesus didn't sniffle, he didn't cry, he wept. I heard a preacher say he only wept because the sisters had so little faith. Baloney. He wept because he loved him. His favorite term for himself was "the Son of man." He saw great beauty in being fully human as well as spiritual. It's one of the things that makes Him so beautiful to me.

Oscar Wilde said, "Where there is sorrow there is holy ground." That holy ground is blessed and consecrated by our honest tears.

Our friends and loved ones who pass from this scene don't want us disabled and paralyzed by long term grief. They know that despair is a greater deceiver than hope.

Get it out, get it over and get on with your life in a way that honors the one you loved.

The Great Transistor Radio Caper

Cliett forgot more about agriculture every morning before he finished his coffee than most men ever know. He taught it at Tyner High School back when they taught important things like that.

He didn't much like it but his students called him "Pappy." It was a title of great respect for us because he looked like every boy's grandfather.

If you thought you were going to put something over on Pappy you were in for seven miles of bad road and forty nights of rain. He was trusting -- as pure and simple as a little child -- but he was not dumb.

Tutt Thompson was the first to learn this. Pappy had a workshop downstairs under the classroom and had his own phone there. When we wanted to go smoke, we'd tell him the phone was ringing and he would say, "Well, go answer it!"

One day Tutt cupped his hand over his ear and said, "Mr. Cliett, I think I hear the phone." He made his usual response and Tutt went out for a smoke and lolled around at least ten minutes. When he returned, Mr. Cliett asked, "Who was that calling, Edgar (Tuff's real name)7" and Tuft said it was just somebody who had the wrong number. Mr. Cliett said, "Ha! I've got you! I had that phone taken out a week ago."

Bill Bacon's loss for trying to outsmart Mr. Cliett was more severe. He had one of the early transistor radios. Those suckers were pretty expensive for a while when they first came out. Bill was proud of his and brought it to class.

All around the classroom Mr. Cliett had built deep book cabinets. Bill got there early and cleared out a place behind the layers of books and turned the radio on so you could just barely hear the music. He asked us to be a part of the plan by telling Mr. Cliett we didn't hear a thing when he asked us about it.

Class started and as Mr. Cliett called the roll, he would stop and listen. Finally he asked, "Where is that music coming from?" We told him we didn't hear a thing. After about the third time, a knowing grin crossed his sweet old happy face. He knew we were trying to outwit him.

He assigned some paper work and as we scratched away, he moseyed around the classroom until he got a fix on the general direction of the music. Methodically he started removing books until he came to the radio. He turned it off and walked to his desk. He opened the right top drawer, placed the radio inside, and locked it.

Bill's plan had been to wait until Mr. Cliett went to lunch and return to the room to dig out his radio. Now it was locked up in Mr. Cliett's desk.

He hung around in the hall for a spell waiting on Mr. Cliett to go to lunch. Then he saw him serenely sitting at his desk eating a sandwich he brought for lunch. Panic-stricken Bill kept peeping around the corner and Mr. Cliett finally asked, "What can I do for you William?"

Afraid to go home without the radio, Bill finally said, "Well, Mr. Cliett, I might as well confess. That was my radio."

"What radio, William?" Mr. Cliett answered.

"You know," Bill answered, his panic in full-bloom by now, "the one back behind all those books."

Mr. Cliett said, "William, I asked the whole class if they heard music and none of you could hear it. None of you knew anything about a radio. I remember well you saying you didn't hear a thing. So don't ever mention anything about a radio to me."

He locked his classroom door and walked away with a grin. No one ever mentioned it again. It took so much wind out of our sails it was a while before we could come up with a sequel to The Great Transistor Radio Caper.